THE HANGING JUDGE

THE HANGING JUDGE

Nowhere, USA Book Four

NINIE HAMMON

STERLING & STONE

Chapter One

VIOLA SAT in the truck out in front of the house, with Essie beside her. On the street, not down the driveway that curved off the street to the front walk, and back out to the street. You a'had to pulled her fingernails out by the roots to get Viola Tackett to admit how excited she was, that she felt like a little kid at Christmas, but unlike the last time she'd stood in front of this house, eaten up with the wanting of it, this time Viola was gonna take what she wanted, take what was owed her! The universe had not done right by Viola Tackett and this was just the beginning of her evening the score.

Esther Ruth was quietly singing the nonsense song she sang almost nonstop from the moment she woke up in the morning until she went to bed at night. They'd all tried, everybody in the family, to figure out where she'd heard it, or even heard something that sounded like it because it wasn't no real song, just one she made up. A lot of the words wasn't even real words, just sounds she could make with that big old tongue, like most people with Down syndrome had, a'sticking out her mouth — ahhh-nah, and gahma-gahma-gahma and so-so-wissy-wheeee. You couldn't rightly say there was a melody, just a kinda sing-song rhythm. If you asked her what the song was about, she'd tuck her chin and get that shy look on her face and say, "'bout nuthin'" and then she'd say sorry, like she done something bad and most times she'd cry. She sounded so pitiful, like a baby rabbit got run over by a tractor, made this wheezy wailing sound, and big old tears would run down her face and drip off her chin. So didn't nobody ask her about the song 'cause didn't nobody want to make the pour little thing cry.

Truth was, she wasn't no little thing, though Viola always thought of her as a little girl. She was a woman growed and didn't bear no resemblance whatsoever to her namesake, the Esther in the Bible who got picked by the king of Persia to be his queen 'cause she was so beautiful. Essie was so fat she waddled when she walked, had a flat, ugly face, round cheeks and almost no hair right on the top of her head, though it did grow thick on the sides and she liked it long, so Viola just let it grow. Viola braided it in big braids that hung all the way to Essie's waist whenever she took her out, which was almost never because the child didn't really care where she was, was happy just a'sittin' in the sunshine grabbin' at dust motes, or splashin' her toes in the creek, singing her song. 'Sides, Essie wasn't completely potty trained and was like to have an accident at any time and didn't nobody want to deal with that.

Viola's brought her along to town today to show Essie her new home.

She'd sent Neb and Obie up to the door to knock while she waited in the truck with Zach and Essie, had to make sure that Mr. Sebastian McFarland Nower III was at home, 'cause she surely did not want to go waltzing in there without being invited. That wasn't a neighborly thing to do and she was all about being neighborly, about treating others with respect. Even if maybe they hadn't never treated her respectful — and they would one day be sorry for that, yes sir they surely would be sorry for a fact.

Neb stepped down off the porch and made come-on motions and Zach started the truck to take his mother and sister right up to the door.

"Drive slow, son," she told him. She was determined to squeeze every bit of the juice of delight from this moment she had been waiting for since she was a little girl.

Viola Tackett was coming home to a place she'd never lived before. Now it was hers, all hers.

There was just the minor detail of Sebastian Nower to contend with but that'd be simple as flicking a fly off'n the end of her nose.

Stepping down out of the truck on the passenger side behind Essie, Viola paused to get her breath, 'cause sitting out there looking at the house had plum knocked the wind out of her.

She didn't know the proper names for the elements of style that made the 150-year-old home such an impressive sight. It was made of red brick, three stories tall and all the windows was tall and thin, and had little ornamental white things over top of them. The ones on the top floor was imbedded in the roof so's the roof tiles come down around them and the second floor was all windows — one after the other, all the way around the house. The first floor had a huge porch, and a roof supported by white pillars.

Even from here, she could see the trim needed a paint job, and a flash of anger blew through her that Sebastian Nower had let the place go like he'd done, hadn't kept it up so's it was a castle, a sight to bless every eye that beheld it.

She could hear Nower's squeaky voice, addressing Neb

like Neb was the butcher selling a pork chop and had tried to put his thumb on the scales.

She walked slowly, regally down the front walk and stepped up onto the porch. Nower was dressed like he'd been at the meeting the night before, a suit and tie. Maybe that's the way he always dressed, didn't never wander around the house in a ratty tee shirt and jeans with holes worn in the butt, or maybe he was getting ready to go to church. It was, after all, Sunday morning, and a body'd ought to have they bum warming a church pew somewhere every Sunday morning. "Remember the Sabbath day to keep it holy." That's what the good book said.

She stopped in front of the suit-and-tie-clad gentlemen standing just inside the house, with the door partially closed.

"Mr. Nower, sounds to me like you didn't quite understand what my oldest boy was telling you."

"I understood every word he said, thank you very much, and I am outraged, offended and ..." He was so flustered he couldn't even hang names on all the ways he was upset. "He says you and your family will be staying here. That's absurd. This is my house and I have not invited you to be my guests. So I will thank you to get off my porch and take your—"

"Now see, there you go. You done already misunderstood what's happening here, Mr. Nower, sir." Her mock graciousness and subservient manner instantly planted a smug smile on his face.

"I knew there had to be some mistake, that—"

"What he didn't make plain was that we ain't moving into this here house as visitors."

Nower was glad for the clarification, but still unsure where the conversation was headed.

"Well, then, I'd appreciate it if you left—"

"We ain't gonna be your guests 'cause *you* ain't gonna be here."

She wanted to laugh out loud at the look of shock on his face. He was so surprised and confused he didn't know what to say, so she strutted her stuff across his porch — *her porch* — and stood in front of him.

"I don't *never* repeat myself, ain't gonna say this but one time so you'd best listen up. I'll use little bitty words so's ain't no way you can misunderstand. If'n you like, I'll wait if you want to go get your crayons so's you can take notes."

He looked at her as if she'd lost her mind and she laughed out loud again. She'd never imagined how much fun this whole thing was going to be.

"I am taking *possession* of this house. As the duly … appointed — as of last night's meeting — judge executive for Nower County, I am confiscating the residence as my home."

"You're *what?* How dare—"

She moved fast for a fat old woman and she was in his face in two steps, grabbed hold of that stupid red tie of his and yanked down so the knife she'd slipped out of a sleeve scabbard was at his throat.

"Here's how I dare, Mr. Nower. I dare because I *can*, and you ain't got no say about it one way or the other because you *can't*. I'm taking this here house to live in. I can't be overseeing the county, be the one who settles disputes and the like, be the "law" from a little old house on Gizzard Ridge in Turkey Neck Hollow … now can I?"

He said nothing, likely couldn't speak.

"I got to be in a place where folks know where I'm at when they got trouble, so they know where to find me. I got to be accessible to the folks I'm sworn I'd protect. So I am taking possession of this house, declaring it … what do the gub-mint call it when it takes your house from you because it's to be used for the good of other folks? The right of eminent domain, that's it. I looked it up."

He just stared at her for a moment, clearly not tracking with what she was saying. After all, he was the upper crust and she was pond scum. Probably wasn't never a single time in his life anybody'd talked to him like this.

"But ... it's *my* house."

"Not anymore it ain't. It's *my* house now, and you got ..." She looked at her watch and then back up into his eyes. "You got half an hour to pack a bag." She turned to her second-born son. "Obie, you go with him, see to it he don't try nothing, help him gather up his clothes and his toothbrush and whatever else he can carry out of here."

"This is ... crazy. Where ... where will I go?"

That statement was a drop of water in hot grease and Viola Tackett only barely kept herself from reaching out and slitting the old man's throat.

"Where will you go? How about somewhere that ain't got no indoor plumbing, somewhere there's an outhouse that stinks. Couple dozen years, though, and you'll get used to the smell, won't seem bad at all. Somewhere it's cold in the wintertime because the wind blows through cracks in the walls, makes the candles flicker on the table. Somewhere there ain't enough food to eat so your belly aches from being hungry."

She noticed his face had gotten red and realized she'd been pulling on his tie as she spoke, drawing it tighter and tighter. She let him go and shoved him away from her and he banged against the wall and almost went down.

"Get your things and get out my house!"

She strode past him through the open door into the foyer and stopped, looking at the polished floors, the curved spindles of the staircase railing as it wound across the wall and up to the second floor, beneath the sparkling chandelier with crystals so bright the flickering light stabbed like little swords into her eyes.

It was the flickering light, that's what done it. Made her eyes water so big tears started running down her cheeks like she was crying. Just the light was all. She could hear Sebastian Nower whining like a little kid as Obie give him the bum's rush toward the back door.

Then she sent the boys out to look under every rock, bush, chicken house and toadstool until they located the fella who was gonna make it clear to the fine citizens of Nowhere County, Kentucky, that Viola Tackett meant business — told them to take him down to that rinky-tink jail and lock him up.

There wasn't nothing in the world good as a public hanging to get the troops in line.

Chapter Two

Jolene Rutherford was surprised there weren't any cars in the Dollar General Store parking lot. There was always somebody there. The poor man's Walmart, which was an oxymoron if Jolene ever heard one. But maybe the store didn't open until nine or ten o'clock and that was hours from now.

She pulled into the lane to her father's house across the road from the store, still unsure what she was going to say to him when they met.

How long had it been? She didn't know, not because she'd just lost count of the years but because she'd never tried to keep track of them in the first place. She didn't want to measure the time she had spent in a "fatherless" … no, "father-*free*" world. Somehow measuring it, qualifying it, made it seem like a situation that needed to be remedied, and she had not been in an emotional space where she had any interest in repairing it — until …

She didn't know why she had been sent her father's medical records. Since the information had been identified as "next of kin" copies, she could only assume that was the reason, but that begged the question *why now?* Even though they had not spoken since … she didn't know when … it wasn't like she had only recently become her father's next of kin.

It appeared to her that she had been sent these particular records because of the information they contained. Cancer. Dying. Okay, it didn't say dying. Didn't have to spell it out. Terms like "in remission" and "regimen of chemotherapy" and "quality of life issues to explore" drew an unmistakable picture.

That's why she had immediately thrown some clothes into a bag in Pittsburgh and set out for Kentucky in the middle of the night. She'd left instructions for the crew to do the preliminary set-up work on the haunted mental institution in West Virginia without her, which, of course, had most certainly left her assistant Cecil Cunningham shouting "Thank you, Jesus"-es and "Now, I get my big chance"-es at the top of his lungs. He wanted her job, was, after all, far more "qualified" than she was, and had not the slightest understanding that the viewers wanted the eggheads to stay eggheads and the nerds to stay nerds. Her fans wanted them to operate the verification equipment and stay out of the way, to interact with the show's host on camera only if she included them in some minor impromptu banter.

Jolene was the reason "If You Got it, Haunt It" was a success. Her personality, her charisma, her charm and wit were the reason people tuned in. Oh yeah, they were fascinated by ghost stories and haunted houses and "investigating paranormal activity." But many a show had come and gone that did those things far better than Jolene did them. The key word being *gone*. She had *stayed*, had lasted because she knew how to work a crowd — even a virtual one on the other side of a television camera. She had earned her chops in that department in a decade of "psychic reading" gigs under a bajillion stage names. This show was the first time she'd used her real name. Jolene. Just Jolene, though. Dropped the Rutherford. Only one name added to the mystery. So did having different "plants" call her "Doctor Jolene" so she could protest with a convincing show of humility: "I've told you, I never turned in my dissertation — was too anxious to get out into the field to do research. So, technically, I am not '*Doctor* Jolene.'"

She was telling the God's own truth. She was not *Dr.* Jolene. She had *not* completed her dissertation. She had not begun it, either. Or a master's thesis. Bachelor's degree, yes, Bachelor of Science in Elementary Education, complete with a teaching certificate. Future laid out before her as clear as the Yellow Brick Road to the Emerald City — get married, teach school, have babies, the American Dream. Trouble was, it wasn't Jolene's dream. And she didn't figure that out until she was a couple of miles down the road — not only didn't go all the way to the Emerald City, but leapt off the road altogether and into the bushes. Consequently, she left some wreckage behind. A failed marriage. A disappointed father.

She had become somebody else entirely in the years after that. Several somebody elses. But a different hairstyle and color now, a pair of glasses, and fifteen pounds lighter and nobody cared enough to link her to all the somebody elses that came before. It appeared that she'd just shown up on the reality television show scene virginal, from academia, a scientist studying the phenomena of paranormal experiences. An objective viewpoint. A neutral observer who had a knack for pulling her viewers into her world, convincing them effortlessly that she wanted to know "the truth" about the subject just as much as they did, that she was partnering with them, that they'd take the journey right alongside her and see together what was on the other side.

Of course, what was on the other side was absolutely nothing. But Jolene understood, as her failed predecessors apparently had not, that everybody *wanted* something to be there. Not anything blatant that would require the High Court of Common Sense to call it into question. Just "something," only enough to leave them wondering. A glimpse of the door with a light shining out beneath it, promising all manner of things on the other side.

That's what she did and she was very good at it, thank you very much. But she had dropped it and everything else in her life and come running back home to Nowhere County, Kentucky because her father was dying.

That's what she wanted to say when she saw him. Only the emotion was bigger than a simple statement. It begged a confrontation, conflict. She wanted to *yell* at him. "Why didn't you tell me you were sick? If I hadn't been forwarded your medical records, I wouldn't have found out there was anything wrong with you until I got a phone call asking me what I wanted them to do with your remains. What a heartless thing to do to your only child!"

She had had many a "shouting conversation" with her father — in her head.

"My choice of a lifestyle and an occupation that doesn't meet with your approval doesn't absolve you of the obligations of simple human decency. Or, is that the point? Your final thumbing your nose at my life is exiting yours without even bothering to say goodbye?"

Saying goodbye.

That's what she had come here for.

She sat for a few minutes in the driveway. Her father's ancient Chevy pickup truck was nowhere in evidence. Not surprising. It had been a classic working its way toward antique-dom even before she left so it was likely nothing more than a pile of rust in some auto salvage yard some- where. But he must have replaced it with some other vehi- cle. Did the empty driveway mean he wasn't home? Or had he parked his whatever in the garage? He *had* to be home. She'd been screwing herself up to seeing him today — *right now* — and it would be miserable to have to wait.

Wait to say what?

It was absurd that she had had all this time to think about it and she still didn't know.

How about, "Hi Dad. I love you."

Maybe now wasn't the time to say all the saved-up-in- anger things she longed to say. Maybe she should respond to her own better instincts, do the kind thing. Make amends and let it be over.

Just say goodbye.

Jolene took a deep breath, got out of the car and walked purposefully up the stone sidewalk to the house, her eyes fixed on the prize. She'd just tell him she loved him. Because despite everything that had happened, she did love him. If she hadn't cared so much she wouldn't have been so devastated by his response to her life.

She whispered the words to herself as she lifted her fist to knock.

"Hi Dad. I love you."

Chapter Three

EIGHT-YEAR-OLD TOBY WITHERSPOON listened to his father banging around in the kitchen as early morning light filtered through his bedroom window, casting shadows on the ceiling. He didn't get up, though, pretended he was still asleep. He wanted to put off facing his father as long as possible because he was certain the man would be in a foul mood this morning. Toby had gotten a good look at his father in the security light over the driveway when his father came home last night. It was obvious that somebody had beaten him up like his father beat his mother — hurt him bad. Oh, how Toby wished he could have watched! He wondered if his father had seen the beating coming, knew what was going to happen before it did.

Toby always knew, always wondered why his mother didn't.

WHY DOESN'T his mother back down, let his father be right, just drop the subject and go on?

But she won't do that and Toby doesn't understand why because it's clear what's going to happen. What always happens when there is that awful tension in the air, like it feels outside sometimes as a thunderstorm rumbles on the other side of the mountain but the first bolt of lightning hasn't struck yet — that awful knowing.

Why doesn't his mother see?

Maybe she does see, but just doesn't care. If that's the case, Toby's mother is either very brave or very dumb. He wants to believe she's brave, just isn't afraid of his father's fists.

But the niggling knowing is there. Not to fear his father's fists is stupid.

Tonight, it's over bananas. His mother is making a salad to take to the get-together she has with some other women where they play some kind of game called Bunco and drink wine and talk about their husbands. Toby hid in the hallway when it was his mother's turn to host the gathering and listened to their conversations. The more wine they drank, the more awful their husbands became.

Except his mother didn't talk about his father and he couldn't understand why not. The things the other women complain about are nothing. Mrs. Sandusky's husband drops cigar ashes on the floor and always has stains on the front of his shirt because he "eats like a pig at a trough." Mrs. Portland's husband sits in front of the television in his underwear, drinking beer and farting and won't take out the trash.

Toby's father beats his mother! Often. It hurts. Oh, he is careful not to damage her face, only that one time when she accused him of going to see a … a prosecute. Toby didn't know what that was but his father smashed his mother's mouth and nose and she stayed in the house for a month and told people she'd been in a car wreck.

She never says anything about it to her friends when they gather to play Bunco, just smiles and says "her Howie" is a good man, a good husband.

When she realizes that her "good husband" has eaten the bananas that were supposed to go into the salad, she asks him to go to the store and get more. He refuses. She says he ate them, he should go get more. He tells her not to push it, that he's had a hard day, a shoplifter in the Dollar General Store.

She says she's had a hard day, too, and that's when he punches her in the stomach.

She doubles over and falls to her knees. Toby wants so badly to go to her defense. To be big and strong enough to protect her. Only once did he try. It earned him a black eye and his mother made him swear he'd never again get between them.

So he watches from where he sits at the table, his dinner of pot roast and mashed potatoes getting cold on his plate.

His father shoves her over onto her side with his foot and she still can't breathe, is doubled over clutching her stomach.

Then he unfastens his belt. Toby wants to cry. He sees the look of fear in his mother's eyes, but he can do nothing.

The strap falls with a horrible slapping sound on her back, and she doesn't cry out because she's not yet recovered from having the breath knocked out of her. She cries out the second time, though, sucks in a big gulp of air and shrieks, but he keeps hitting her, doesn't fear the neighbors will hear because there's only Mr. Hayes and he's deaf.

She curls up in a ball, and still he hits her. On her back and her butt and her upper legs. Places nobody can see. Toby knows that later tonight when she sits together with her friends drinking wine and playing cards, that she will say she's moving slow because she's sore from working too hard in the garden.

And they'll believe her.

TOBY WONDERED what story his father was going to tell people to explain his injuries, though maybe he'd just admit he'd been in a fight. His mother always lied to people, covered up because … yeah, because what? Did she not want to get his father in trouble? Or was she just embarrassed to admit he was a monster?

Maybe his father would just tell the truth, but Toby

didn't think he would because if he'd been in a fight, he had lost, and he probably wouldn't want to admit that. Somebody clawed his cheek, hit him in the face hard enough to break his nose, bust his lip and maybe break some teeth. His hand had been bleeding. And his father had probably hurt the other guy, too, and neither one of them could go to the emergency room to get patched up because of the Jabberwock.

Toby tried to grab hold of the next thoughts but they got away from him, leapt out of his grasp as they always did and he could never catch them. He never allowed himself to think about the Jabberwock because J-Day had been the last time he had ever seen his mother. And he *had* seen her that day. She had been *here* … not in Lexington. His father told people she had got trapped outside the Jabberwock and that's why she didn't come home. But that was a lie. It wasn't the Jabberwock that kept her away. His mother didn't come home because …

She was dead. And his father had killed her.

The truth of that elbowed its way out of the recesses of Toby's mind and stood in the center in a bright spotlight, demanding his attention. And he gave up, stopped fighting it — the truth was always stronger than he was. It was a ritual he had gone through every day for almost two weeks. He would refuse to let himself know his father had killed his mother, wrestle with the truth of it. But he always lost and when he did he'd set out yet again scouring the house, looking for … he didn't know what — just "proof" that his father was a murderer. He never found any, though, and who would he tell if he did?

Who was there left to enforce the law, to hold anybody accountable for breaking it? Toby didn't know. He only knew he had to find *somebody* to care. Somewhere. Had to find *evidence*! Cop shows were very definite about that part. As soon as Toby had evidence, they would come and lock his father away for the rest of his life.

Chapter Four

JOLENE KNOCKED on the door of her father's house but no one answered. Maybe he was gone to one of his chemotherapy appointments.

Chemotherapy.

Cancer.

She lifted her hand and knocked again, louder. Nothing but silence from inside. After a third unanswered knock, she tried to knob ... and it wasn't locked. No big surprise. The doors had never been locked when she was a child. But still. It was 1995 and hard to believe there was somewhere in America where people didn't lock their doors at night.

Opening the door just far enough that she could call out, "Hello, hello. Anybody home? Avon calling."

No response.

"Actually, I'm selling Girl Scout cookies and I can get you a great discount on snickerdoodles."

Nothing.

She opened the door all the way but didn't step inside because ...

Yeah, because why?

Because she had suddenly begun to feel inexplicably anxious. Apprehensive. Her heart rate increased for no apparent reason.

"Dad," she called out through the open door into a small foyer.

Her father had built this house after he retired, had apparently wanted to be the lone resident of the Middle of Nowhere. She hadn't been consulted, given that they never talked, and she wasn't sure why he had decided to move from their home in the North Fork Valley on the other side of the Wiley Bridge. In the early 1980s, the historic covered bridge had been declared unsafe for vehicles over 15,000 pounds, so she and the other children who rode a bus across it to school in Persimmon Ridge had to get out on one side of the bridge, wait for the bus to cross, then walk across on foot and get back aboard.

"I'm from the Publisher's Clearing House with your check for a million dollars, and if you don't claim it …"

Silence.

Clearly, no one was home.

But that was the thing — it *felt* like somebody was there. The air was heavy, stuffy. Even standing outside with the door wide open, it didn't feel like there was enough air in the room.

"Dad?"

Silence gobbled up the word.

The plaintive, little-girl quality of her voice struck her and she realized she actually sounded, well, not scared, but at least creeped out.

What was wrong with her?

She forced herself to step into the house, but she didn't close the door behind her and she didn't like that she was *unwilling* to close the door behind her.

Two steps into the foyer where she could see into the other rooms of the house and she understood why nobody had answered. Nobody lived here. The dining room was bare, not a stick of furniture, nothing but a mirror and an old painting of a lighthouse in a storm on the wall. There'd been a lighthouse picture over the mantle in the house where she grew up — was it this one? She could see into the living room and kitchen from where she stood and there was no furniture there, either. Had she gotten the address wrong?

A sudden panic closed her throat — was she too late? Had her father died already? Fear threatened to carry her away but she made herself calm down. He'd been "stable" when he'd gone in for the checkup that had generated the next-of-kin report, with a prognosis of "months of treatment." If he'd died, they'd have notified her. And they certainly wouldn't have cleaned out his house without her consent.

She didn't like that she had to force herself to walk farther into the house, and certainly didn't like that every step was more difficult than the last. It was the odd feeling of … okay, call it what it was. The feeling of *opposition*. Like she somehow was not supposed to be here and was definitely not only uninvited but unwelcome.

When she walked into the living room, she stopped in her tracks and stared, shocked by what occupied one whole wall. It was a hand-drawn map of Nower County. But more than a mere map. It didn't just have road names, creeks and mountains, towns and rivers. It had … *everything*. She approached it in something like reverence. The detail was stunning. The kind of details only a lifelong mailman would know. Her father had made this map. She was sure of it. No one else could have done it and there was no telling how many hours her father had devoted to the creation of it.

So this *was* her father's house!

Then why wasn't there any furniture in it?

Why had he left the map on the wall when he moved out?

And where was her father, the man who had spent — how long? Decades, surely — drawing that map?

In truth, what else did he have to do? Unless he had taken up golf or tennis in his old age, he'd had to come up with something to fill the hours of every day after he retired. He'd never liked movies and hated television, would turn it off when he came into the room even when she was watching a show. She'd get up, turn it back on, and he'd roll his eyes and curl up in a chair with his newspaper.

Which was why she was certain he hadn't seen *If You've Got it, Haunt It*. He hadn't likely seen any television show since she left for college. Even if he'd had a set, he wouldn't have tuned in to *that* show. Why would he watch a show dedicated to tricking people? Why would he watch a "charlatan" play on people's fears? Why would he watch a conman? Or in her case, a con-woman?

And that's what he'd thought of her profession after she gave up the Little Miss Perfect job of teaching second grade and had dumped Little Miss Perfect's perfect husband and became a psychic reader.

He'd thought she was a swindling fraud even before she started ghost hunting. In fact, he didn't need to know anything more about how she lived her life than her profession to bestow upon her his unequivocal disapproval.

Game over.

But studying the map he had obviously spent years creating, she couldn't help feeling sorry for him. The people who lived here didn't care enough to keep their towns incorporated. They would cheerfully have moved away to somewhere that mattered if they could. Yet her father had "immortalized nowhere" with meticulous care in splendid detail.

It was hard to think of anything more pathetic.

"Pitiful," she said aloud. And her breath frosted in front of her.

When — *how?* — had it gotten cold? Between one heartbeat and the next the air had turned frigid. The sun had risen behind a gray overcast sky this morning, but it was *summertime* outside. She shivered violently. The end of her nose felt frozen. Her body was covered in goosebumps. She shouldn't be here.

Shouldn't be here? Why not?

She should leave now. Right now.

Why?

Because you don't belong here.

True that. This was her father's house, not the home where she had grown up. It belonged to him and …

Who said she didn't belong here?

The words were ringing in her head as if they had been spoken aloud. But there wasn't anybody here. She looked around — at nothing in an empty room.

Nothing. Empty. Yet she was filled with an unshakeable belief that she was not alone. That there was somebody … or some*thing* … Something very cold. As cold as death.

Was that … it couldn't be frost on the walls.

Frost. On the walls. It sparkled like glitter.

She closed her eyes, opened them again slowly. No frost. Thank God! She'd been holding her breath and she let it out in a whoosh. For an instant, it became a puff of white vapor in front of her face. She gasped the air back in, held it, not moving … and watched in fascinated horror as a second puff of white vapor formed in front of her, *as if somebody else were standing there, breathing out.*

Now *that* was lunacy. Absolutely, industrial-strength bull-goose crazy.

She was falling for her own fantasy, the one she made up for other people. There was no such thing … as …

She refused even to think the word *ghost*. There was no such thing — if anybody knew that it was Jolene Rutherford. And even if there were ghosts — there weren't, there really weren't — but even if there *were*, ghosts were dead people and her father was alive.

He was alive, wasn't he?

She only knew that as the default answer. As his next of kin, she hadn't been notified, ergo: he was fine.

He was not dead.

He was not a ghost

There was no "ghost" in this house.

No entity emanating cold, telling her she had no right to be here, breathing—

Bam!

Jolene jumped when the front door banged shut behind her, came as close as she had ever been to wetting her pants.

The wind slammed it shut, of course.

There was no wind. Not even a breeze. The leaves on the trees had been still.

The sense of oppression, of closeness, grew with every breath. The sense that there was *too much* in the room, not enough air to breathe, that somebody or some*thing* wanted her *gone!*

She began backing out of the room, then let her fear loose, couldn't hold onto it a second longer. She turned and bolted away from the pitiful map, had to get out of the house that was her father's where she wasn't welcome.

She grabbed the doorknob of the front door that had just slammed.

The door wouldn't open. It was locked.

The world got screwy for Jolene Rutherford after that.

When she tried to piece the sequence of events together as she sat in the Dollar General Store parking lot hyperventilating, not really sure how she had gotten there, she couldn't put things in chronological order.

Forcing herself to stop gasping — it had felt like she was suffocating in there — she gripped the steering wheel so tight her fingers turned white. Gritted her teeth.

Calm. Down.

Breathe.

Just *breathe!*

In.

Out. Exhale slowly.

And as normal sensations, normal thoughts, common sense, and *reality* reasserted themselves, Jolene Rutherford could not believe she was sitting here like this.

She had come home to see her father. He wasn't home. She went inside, saw a map he had drawn and then … left.

How had circumstances so simple and innocent grown into such gothic proportions? How had the whole thing degenerated into such fear? Not fear, terror.

Because that was the killer, the coup de grâce, the whole enchilada. Jolene, the vampire slayer, okay the ghost hunter, had been scared spit-less. The whole time she was in her father's house, from the moment she shoved the door into the room and stepped inside.

The *unlocked* door. It had been unlocked.

So why was it locked when she tried to leave? When she was scrambling, scratching to get it open, her trembling fingers unable to operate the simple deadbolt mechanism to—

Deadbolt.

A door handle lock could conceivably engage if the door were slammed hard enough. Conceivably. Unlikely, but possible. But a deadbolt? The door slammed and the deadbolt engaged. That was insane, impossible.

But it had happened.

It had … hadn't it?

"Okay, stop it."

She said the words aloud and as she did she realized her throat was raw and then she remembered screaming, so loud and long that it had made her hoarse.

Nothing that was happening right now made any sense!

Another car pulled into the parking lot, a red Lexus, and she registered again that the place was certainly empty as Dollar General Store parking lots went. There were two men in the car. Both black, one young and good-looking, the other old and … familiar, somehow. They didn't pull into one of the many open, unoccupied spaces in front of the door. The car pulled up beside her and the old man who was on the passenger side rolled down his window.

"Lo there," he said.

"Hello," she said tentatively. There was something about him she recognized. "Mr. … *Jackson?* Is that you, Mr. Jackson? Remember me, Jolene Rutherford? I was in your freshman math class."

"Jolene, why yes. How are you?"

"How am I?" She blurted out a bleat of inappropriate laughter and noted that a knowing look passed between the two men.

"I came to visit my father but he wasn't home."

"Neither is anybody else in Nower County," Mr. Jackson said.

Chapter Five

STUART MCCLINTOCK and Cotton Jackson pulled to a stop on County Road 278 at the crossroads in the Middle of Nowhere. Lack of sleep had dumped a truckload of gravel in Stuart's eyes. He'd gotten very little the night before he arrived in Nowhere County and almost none last night on the lumpy cot at Cotton's house. Neither of them had gone back to bed after awful nightmares jarred them awake in the middle of the night, so they'd set out early this morning. Cotton had said he wanted to take a look at the hole Reece Tibbits had blown in the road, but now that sightseeing tour was shoved to the back burner. There was a van parked in front of the Dollar General Store. The words emblazoned on the side of the van would have peaked Stuart's curiosity no matter where the vehicle had been parked. But here in the Middle of Nowhere? And *now* — when the whole of Nower County was MIA — well, Stuart heard the theme song from *The Twilight Zone* begin to play softly in his head.

"If You've Got It, Haunt It," the words proclaimed,

the title of the hit reality television show about … paranormal activity. Ghost hunting.

He and Cotton exchanged a look, and Stuart wordlessly turned off the road and into the parking lot, pulled into the parking space beside the van and Cotton rolled down his window.

The driver of the van was "Jolene," the host of the show, who just happened to be, oh by the way, a former student of Cotton's.

Stuart listened to their conversation, marveling that the woman who had the highest-rated reality television show on the air actually hailed from Nower County, Kentucky. And so did the woman who had written — arguably — the most famous series of children's books since Harry Potter. Both from this one place, this one forgettable nowhere place. How likely was a thing like that?

He was considering that and missed the conversational cue.

"Ahem," said Cotton, too loud. "And this is Stuart McClintock. He is married to Charlie Ryan; do you remember her?"

"I remember the name. Her mother taught ceramics classes, didn't she? She was five years younger than me so I was out of high school before she started." This was the point where you extended your hand, only that was impossible when people in separate cars were introduced. She settled for, "Good to meet you, Mr. McClintock."

"Stuart."

"Okay, Stuart."

Stuart cut to the chase.

"Your father isn't home, you said? Is that right?"

"Right … not home. I'm … waiting for him."

"In the Dollar Store parking lot?" Stuart asked, and got

what he was looking for, the startle, the shock covered up. He was proud of himself that he'd caught it. A professional con artist like Jolene would have had lots of practice hiding her emotional responses and body language from other people.

"Well, I came here because …"

"You suddenly felt an insatiable desire for a RC Cola and a moon pie?" Cotton offered.

Jolene smiled. "Well, true, I haven't had either one of those in a long time."

"You get back here often to see your father?" Stuart asked.

"No, actually I don't. Haven't been here in years."

She'd closed up when he asked that, sensitive subject. He got that. He'd rather not have to dig up the reason it'd taken him two weeks to go looking for Charlie and Merrie. Nobody wanted to discuss emotional wounds with strangers.

"It was nice to meet you, gentlemen," Jolene said, clearly about to end the conversation as if she were going back to her father's house to wait for him.

Stuart thought about how he had felt in Charlie's house, the closeness, the not-enough-air, the sense of you're-not-welcome-here that had driven him away. You don't suppose …

"You're not going back to your father's house to wait for him, are you?" He asked the question direct and blunt, like he'd drop an unexpected question on a hostile witness on the stand, watched her eyes. She squinted. Bingo, he'd hit a nerve.

"Actually, I'm thinking about going back at least as far as Richmond and getting a room. I drove through the night to get here and—"

"You blew by what Cotton said when we drove up. Let me repeat it for you. You said your father wasn't home and

Cotton said, 'neither is anybody else in Nower County.' Aren't you curious what he meant by that?'"

"What's there to mean? That's like saying there's an idiot in Congress and somebody pointing out there's nobody in Congress who isn't. Just something you say."

"He meant it." Stuart strained out all emotion from the statement. "There really isn't anybody in Nower County."

Of course, she had no idea what he was talking about. How could they possibly ... the same way Cotton had convinced him — a picture was worth a thousand words. He gave the older man a nudge and he took the handoff like a pro.

"Jolene, would you mind doing an old man a favor?"

You could see she was ready to be shed of them both, but he'd put her on the spot.

"I'd be glad to help you if I can, Mr. Jackson."

"It's Cotton, not 'Mr. Jackson.'"

"Not sure I'll be able to call my math teacher by his first name, but I'll give it a shot. What can I do for you?"

"Take a little ride with me." He held up his hand to ward off a protest before she had time to raise it. "I promise it won't take half an hour. We're just going to drive into the Ridge and back. You can leave your van here."

"But what for? Why—?"

"Just humor me, will you? Please. I'm an old man, getting older by the minute. If I recall, it was your class of students that started the aging process. Nobody was interested in tackling calculus at fifteen when they intended to drop out of school at sixteen." He paused. "If I recall, math wasn't your strong suit, either."

She gave a weak smile. "Busted. I never was much for facts and figures." Stuart could see she was stalling, trying to think up some excuse to decline Cotton's request, and apparently coming up empty.

"Please …"

"Okay, sure, I will take a little ride with you if you'll promise me one thing?"

"Anything."

"No math problems."

"Actually, we are solving a problem of sorts, but it isn't mathematical."

Cotton opened his door, got out and offered her his seat to ride shotgun.

Stuart was silent as they drove along, not really listening to the banal conversation between Cotton and Jolene, wondering how a woman like her would take the realization that … as Shakespeare put it, "There are more things in heaven and earth than are dreamt of in your philosophy."

Jolene Rutherford wasn't a pretty woman, but she managed to make the best of what she had to work with. Thick eyebrows over large brown eyes that protruded just a little, not the bug-eyed look of people with thyroid problems, just enough to be noticeable. Her nose was thin and sharp, severe, but her wide mouth and full lips granted it some reprieve. All the features individually should have been granted a "pretty" designation, but put them all together and the whole was somehow less than the sum of the parts, thinking mathematically.

Cotton was pointing out houses to her as they drove along. One old house after another.

"I don't remember that many ancient — wait a minute." They had just passed a falling-down shack and she turned around to look at it as they pulled away. "That's not an old house; well, not as old as it looks. Maxine Bailey and I hung out together in high school and her father built that house. They moved in when we were juniors. How on earth did it age that much in less than a couple of decades?"

"They all have," Cotton said.

"All have what?"

"All the houses, the old ones. Two weeks ago they were just like your remember the Bailey family's house."

Clearly, she wasn't tracking.

"Let's say they haven't been old long," Stuart said.

"I have no idea what you're talking about."

"I know you don't," Cotton said. "But you will."

They drove into the Ridge, down the empty streets, past Peetree's Hardware where the front door still stood open. You could see into the building through it, and through the plate glass windows on some of the other buildings, could see there was nothing inside. No people, nothing.

Stuart watched Jolene's face change from curiosity to surprise, to concern, saw she was edging toward freaking out.

"Where is ... everybody?" She tried to make the question light and emotionless but couldn't pull it off. "They all go to a party and we weren't invited?"

"I doubt they're at a party," Stuart said. "Wherever they went, I doubt it was by invitation."

Jolene turned to him, shot a look at Cotton in the backseat, then let her apprehension come out as anger.

"What's with all the creepy veiled references? What are you guys selling?"

"Pull in here," Cotton instructed Stuart, indicating one of the multitude of empty spaces on the street in front of Willingham's Drug Store. "Let's have a soda and talk about it."

Without giving her time to protest, he got out of the

car and started toward the door that Stuart could see was slightly ajar.

"I've come here several times in the past couple weeks. Left some paper cups. There's no ice cream in the freezer, but the wall spigots still work so you can have a soft drink."

He held the door open for her and after a moment's hesitation, she went in. Stuart followed.

The soda counter was still there, as were the stools attached to the floor. Otherwise, the building was empty, no shelves, no merchandise, nothing. There were wall shelves which should have been jammed with women's foofy products.

Maybelline, L'Oréal, Cover Girl — the signs remained but there was nothing on the shelves beneath them. Or on the shelves where there would have been heating pads, greeting cards, candy, vitamins, cold remedies or insoles.

Looked like the business had conducted an extremely successful going-out-of-business sale … "everything must go!"

A stack of paper cups sat on the counter and Cotton picked up one, stepped to a spigot on the back wall and began to fill it with liquid.

"Machine doesn't work or I'd make you a root beer float with that soft serve stuff that doesn't have a speck of anything organic in it, dairy or otherwise. Just some kind of petroleum product."

She had had it.

"Alright, what is going on? Stop the word games, the knowing looks, the veiled references, the spooky hints. Why did you bring me here?"

"A picture's worth a thousand words," Stuart said simply.

"Only way we'd ever convince you that everybody in

Nower County really has vanished is to show you. You'd never have believed us if we'd just told you."

"Vanished?"

Stuart noticed that he and Cotton were nodding their heads like bobblehead dolls and he stopped.

"Have a seat," Cotton said, indicating one of the floor-mounted stools. She sat — reluctantly.

"I flew in yesterday from Chicago to Lexington and rented that car." Stuart nodded toward the Lexus parked out front. "I came to find my wife, Charlie, and my little girl." He was surprised that his voice was suddenly tear-clotted. "She's three. Her name's Merrie. Not Mary, as in Mary had a little lamb, but Merrie, like the hobbit from *Lord of the Rings*." He stopped, gathered himself. "But they weren't here. Just like your father, and Cotton's wife, Thelma, and every other man, woman and child in Nower County ... they have vanished."

Chapter Six

MALACHI WOKE up in the woods, aware from the soreness in his bones, the dew on his chest and the twigs in his hair that he had spent the night there. He sat bolt upright and almost clocked himself with a broken-off branch of the tree he'd slept under. He squinted, got a good look at it and groaned. A fruitless mulberry tree — better described as a big, homely weed, a gawky hunk of poor-quality wood and ugly leaves, that always kept on hand a supply of dead limbs ready to drop on people, cars or roadside utility lines.

It was fitting that he'd spent the night beneath its unlovely boughs.

He had better sense than to shake his head to clear it, just eased back down onto the ground lumpy with the ugly tree's protruding roots and looked up at a sky not far gone past dawn.

Though it was clear he'd spent the night in the woods, what wasn't clear was why he'd taken refuge here. Searching through the scattered random-firing synapses of his mind, he looked for what he had been doing before his life, mind and body had been hijacked by PTSD and transported somewhere else as surely — though with less of a hangover afterward — as the Jabberwock did those who dared to try to leave Nowhere County.

He sat up slowly this time, looked around. He had been digging in the rubble of a house ... The image of two identical faces formed before him. The Tungate brothers. He had been helping Roscoe Tungate search for his brother Harry, who was ... *gone*. Gone in the same way Abner Riley had been gone.

So where was Roscoe?

Why had Malachi gone running off into the woods?

He didn't remember why specifically, only knew that he'd spent the past ... however many hours, fighting ghosts in imaginary battles in the woods of Kentucky, that he'd believed were the rainforests of Rwanda.

When he *was supposed to be* attending the county meeting with Charlie and Sam. He had been selected to deliver the message.

"You do it, Malachi," one of them had said — either Sam or Charlie. "People won't try to shoot the messenger if you do it."

And the message was simple and bleak: get your heads out of your backsides, people, and recognize that your chief problem is NOT surviving somehow inside the Jabberwock bubble until it blows away. The Jabberwock has even more heinous plans than keeping a terrarium of humans in Nowhere County. Unless we figure out what this thing is and how to get rid of it, the Jabberwock is going to take us all — one by one — absorb us or whatever it is the beast does to people like Roscoe Tungate and Abner Riley. If we don't figure it out, we will vanish. If we don't figure it out quick, E.J. will die of rabies.

He had missed the meeting.

He was sure either Sam or Charlie had taken over for

him. He owed them an apology and an explanation — that he had finally stumbled into it, the black hole in his memories he'd been avoiding ever since he left Rwanda. He knew now what had happened there, how he'd gotten the leg wound that had ended his military career. He had spent the night in the woods reliving that horror. The replay had brought its own kind of healing, if that's what you wanted to call it. He had been running from the memory of a horror he had been unable to prevent. A savage brutality he'd been powerless to oppose. Understanding that was both a comfort and a new kind of awful.

Somehow what he was doing now seemed like a mirror image. He was fighting a nightmare horror he couldn't see, whose motives he couldn't understand, but whose intent was clear — to kill everybody in the county. That's what the Hutus had been doing — their objective had been to rid the world of the Tutsis and they had shown no mercy, given no quarter.

Neither would the Jabberwock.

An hour of explanations and half a dozen soft drinks later, Jolene Rutherford was still unconvinced. Oh, something was going on. Something exceedingly weird. That was obvious. But vanished? She wasn't buying.

It wasn't until Stuart started telling her about his experience in Charlie's mother's house that interest sparked in her eyes. She asked questions — would have made a good trial lawyer because she came at the same point from different directions, dug for details, made him repeat his description of the sensation of breathlessness, of heaviness in the air, the sense that the empty room was somehow too crowded. When he'd said he had a clear perception that he was an intruder, an uninvited and unwanted guest, her face went pale.

"I ran out of there," he said, and the mere memory of it tightened his gut in a fist of fear. "I not only didn't lock the back door, I think I left it wide open, just leapt into my car and—"

"So did I," Jolene said.

"So did you what?"

She considered before she spoke, clearly didn't want to share what had happened to her because to do so would put her on "their side."

"I ran out, leapt into my van and drove away. That was mostly a reaction to the fact that the door slammed and locked," she paused, looked at them both pointedly before she continued, "*by itself*, and my hands were shaking so bad I had trouble getting the deadbolt to disengage so I could get out of there."

There was belief in her eyes now, reluctant — but who wouldn't be reluctant? It was obvious that she no longer thought they were making things up.

"It's … real," she said and barked out a bleat of inappropriate laughter as wonder spread across her face. Then she burst out laughing in earnest and leapt to her feet. "It's real. All the crap I have been faking for years … for my whole career. It's *real*. There really are ghosts."

"What's happening here isn't about ghosts!" Stuart said. Because ghosts were the spirits of the dead and Charlie and Merrie were not dead!

"Of course it is." Jolene blew by his remark. "Trust me, I know a ghost when I see one." She giggled again. "Were they really there all along, in all the places I went, but I just couldn't see them?"

"You're reading this all wrong," Stuart said. "I know,

with your frame of reference, you would jump to the conclusion that the … unnatural—"

"Supernatural."

"Okay, supernatural phenomena we've been experiencing here might look similar—"

"Similar? Oh, this is way more than 'similar.' What you described, Stuart, the phenomena in Charlie's house, and what happened to me in my father's house — those were *ghosts*. I am an expert on ghosts." She looked at them a bit sheepishly. "You can't fake the real thing convincingly unless you know what the real thing is."

Then her face lit up like a flare had gone off behind her eyes.

"The equipment. I have it! It was loaded in the back of the van and I didn't unload it, just brought it with me."

"Equipment?" Cotton had never seen Jolene's television show and didn't know she was talking about the gadgets and gizmos that were supposed to "measure" paranormal activity. Smoke and mirrors.

She turned to Stuart. "I didn't get to be one of the best 'psychics' on the circuit without learning to read body language. Yours is so loud it's shouting at me. You think those machines are nothing but—"

"Smoke and mirrors?"

"Let me give you a little lesson in ghostbusting. A GaussMaster EMF meter *really does* measure electromagnetic fields. I have all four types of motion sensors — passive infrared, ultrasonic, microwave and tomographic — that detect motion in complete darkness, infrared thermometers to measure surface temperature, the latest model geophone that converts surface vibrations into voltage which can be recorded …"

She caught the skepticism in his look.

"Hey, you guys wanted me to take what you're selling

on face value, you need to extend me the same courtesy." She looked intently at Stuart. "The machines are *real*. They are honest science. They work. It's just that … let's say we're talking about a simple set of scales. You've tested it, know that it weighs accurately, so you give it to me to use on my show — an apparatus that's nothing more than an objective dispenser of information. But it can still report the wrong weight *if somebody's thumb is on the scales.* That's what I do, what I've been doing for years. I put my thumb on the scales. Make it appear the objective machines really did pick up something. Not a huge win, not a slam dunk, not *holy crap that's a ghost floating up there on the ceiling!* But enough activity to leave the viewer with some hope their long-held belief that the dead really are trying to communicate is real."

She leaned closer.

"The machines are as objective as scales; they *work*. We can use them here, now. We can measure *real* psychic activity, get factual data that's scientifically verifiable."

"So you're telling me that you believe your father is *dead?*"

She winced at that. Good.

"That he has returned to his house to haunt it, that his ghost is—?"

"No, that's *not* what I'm saying! There are other explanations for the disappearance of all these people that aren't based on them all being dead. I don't believe the whole county — how many people?"

Stuart and Cotton looked at each other and spoke in unison.

"Nobody knows," Cotton said.

"There doesn't seem to be a number," Stuart said.

"Well, however many of them there are — they didn't all get killed by some plague that dissolves people *and* all their belongings. All those people are alive — *somewhere*. I am not saying that the presence you sensed in Charlie's mother's house and what I sensed in my father's were *their* ghosts, the spirits that have left their *dead bodies*. What I am saying is that what we encountered were ghosts — *not theirs, but somebody's*."

She looked from one to the other of them. "And I intend to prove it."

Chapter Seven

WHEN CHARLIE LOOKED up and saw Malachi standing in the doorway of E.J.'s room, a wave of hostility washed over her so hot he surely must have felt the heat fifteen feet away.

E.J. was asleep, courtesy of one of the best pain medications ever put on the market, oxycontin, available courtesy of some illegal drug enterprise she hadn't asked Malachi about — because there were some things in life you were better off not knowing. Malachi's whole family was engaged in one criminal endeavor or another, had always been and would likely always be — so the least he could do was filch some of their larder to ease the real pain of his friend.

If, indeed, Malachi Tackett was anybody's friend.

It appeared he had read some if not all of what Charlie was thinking from the look on her face, but did not look chagrined. If anything, he looked empathetic, like he understood how somebody would feel enmity toward him and his family — you know, given that they were drug dealers, thieves, murderers and all that — so he didn't begrudge her some hard feelings.

That made Charlie even angrier.

Then she heard Sam's voice from out in the hallway.

"Malachi! Where have you been?"

There was no accusation in Sam's tone, only concern, and it wasn't until then that Charlie noticed his appearance — disheveled, dirty and with that horrible haunted look in his eyes. It was a look that said wherever you'd been that you thought was worse than where he'd been, he'd see your monster and raise you ten. And whatever it was you were thinking he'd done, he'd actually done ten times worse.

The anger drained out of Charlie. He wasn't responsible for what his family had done — much of it while he was serving his country getting his butt shot off on some foreign battlefield. But she was massively disappointed and she was sure that showed, too. She had counted on him. So had Sam. And so had Liam.

He had let all of them down.

He started to speak, but Charlie put her finger to her lips and got quietly out of the chair and came to the door of E.J.'s room. She and Sam had been reluctant to leave his side. The low-grade fever he'd been running since he'd been mauled by a rabid dog on Friday had blossomed into a full-bore fever of almost 101 degrees. It bespoke infection, but Sam could find no evidence of it in his mangled wound. There was nothing to do but to pump him full of antibiotics. Gratefully, there was no scarcity of those — yet! — because the animal hospital had been well stocked with basic medications that, with some study and some math, could be used for humans as well.

"Rusty can stay with him for a little while," Sam said, and beckoned her son, who was actually reading a book to

Merrie in the waiting room. Both Charlie and Sam had brought their children with them to the veterinary/people clinic for their shifts with E.J. Neither would admit to being reluctant to let their offspring out of their sight, but that was the reason. Rusty had proven to be a surprisingly good babysitter for Merrie — mainly because he loved to read and she loved to be read to, even if she couldn't understand the story. And with the menagerie of animals to be tended to, there was enough to keep both of them occupied.

Rusty took Sam's place in the chair beside E.J.'s bed. Merrie went to help Raylynn feed the puppies and Sam led the parade down the hallway, with Malachi behind her and Charlie bringing up the rear. They went into the break-room at the end of the hall; Charlie closed the door behind them and then leaned against it, her eyes closed.

"Liam's dead," Malachi said with no discernible emotion in his voice. Charlie opened her eyes and he was looking at her when he said it. She felt a hammer blow of sorrow. "I caught a ride into town with Billy Dan Singleton — in his brother's truck." Billy Dan had tried to blast his way through the Jabberwock with his souped-up Chevy. "He was at the meeting last night."

"Did he tell you what happened?" Charlie asked, challenge in her voice but she didn't care. "How your mother and brothers staged a coup right there in the school auditorium, took over the whole county lock, stock and barrel — we're running things now, thank you very much. If you have a problem, see Viola Tackett. I'm not sure if you have to kiss her ring."

"And you think I knew she was going to do that?"

"I figured that's why you neglected to show up."

"Chai ... there's more," Sam said, not looking at him but studying the tiles on the floor near her feet. Chai.

Charlie had heard Sam call Malachi that before, almost a term of endearment.

"Before we pour more gasoline on the fire, let's deal with the blaze we have going already." Pulling out a chair, Malachi flipped it around, straddled the seat and laid his forearms on the back. He included Sam in his explanation, but it felt to Charlie like it was directed at her, and she wondered if Billy Dan had told him about her little speech, and how what she had said had ruffled the queen hen's feathers. "I was not at the meeting because … I was fighting other battles. That weren't real." He rested his forehead briefly on his forearms. "I don't know what happened or where I was exactly. I'm still piecing it together."

"You left with Roscoe to go to Harry's to see what happened to him," Charlie said.

"And nobody's seen either one of you again after that," Sam said.

Malachi's head snapped up.

"Roscoe? You saying Roscoe didn't come back to town?"

Sam shook her head.

"Has anybody …" You could tell he didn't want to continue. "Has anybody been out to Roscoe's place to check on him?"

Charlie shot Sam a startled look.

"*You* don't know where he—?"

"Harry's house was … falling down. Like the others, aged a century. Roscoe jumped out of the truck, started digging around, trying … like maybe he'd find Harry under a rock. When he saw I wasn't digging, he told me to go back to the truck."

He took a deep breath.

"And the next thing I knew I was in Rwanda with my

sergeant ordering me back to the truck so a tribe of butchers could massacre a family … and chop off a little boy's head as a gift for me."

Obviously, he hadn't intended to say all that and seemed a little surprised that he had.

He took a breath.

"The next thing I knew I was lying under a stupid mulberry tree. What happened between the time I left Roscoe and when I woke up … I have absolutely no idea."

"Roscoe didn't go looking for—?"

"I don't know what Roscoe did or didn't do. All I know is that when I got back to Harry's house … what was left of Harry's house, Roscoe was gone and I had to hike over Callahan Mountain to Crocket Pike to hitch a ride."

"Roscoe didn't come back into town," Sam said.

Malachi dropped his forehead back on his forearms. "My guess is you can cross his name off your Christmas card list."

He lifted his head and saw the shocked looks on their faces and could only muster a tired, "Sorry. Inappropriate black humor. My bad. What I'm saying is that I think I know what we'll find when we go out to Roscoe's house."

He turned back to Sam then and asked, "Okay, what's the 'more' you want to tell me about Liam getting shot?"

Sam hooked his eyes with hers. Didn't flinch. Charlie was proud of her.

"Your mother killed him."

STUART MCCLINTOCK LOOKED across the table at Cotton Jackson's weary face and acknowledged that his own face likely looked just as exhausted and haggard. They hadn't gone back to bed after they'd both awakened in the grip of horrific nightmares, courtesy of whatever it was that flat out did not want them sticking their nose into its business. That lost sleep piled on top of the sleepless nights Stuart had spent before he ever got to Nowhere County weighed him down and made it hard to think.

Only Jolene was rested. No, not just rested — so full of energy it pulsed off her like sparks off a blown transformer. She was exuberant, excited by the possibility that she might actually encounter real paranormal activity.

That prospect didn't excite Stuart. It yanked his gut into a knot of dread.

He sat quietly, not really listening as she described the functions of the equipment she had packed away in her van, the one with the name of her television show embla-zoned on the side. It was ghost tracking equipment, and from what he could gather, it was moderately sophisticated scientific gear that she'd used to find the boogeyman in the closet in homes from Bangor to Bakersfield, Sarasota to Seattle — and to make her show a household name all over the country.

He was too tired, too worried and too … okay, admit it, too frightened to pull punches, to sugarcoat reality, to be polite.

"Your show is a fraud and you're a shyster." He held up his hand in an appeasing gesture when her face flushed. "An entertaining fraud, and a charming shyster — I get it. You're not looking for reality, just trying to amuse your audience. And there's not a thing wrong with that. But hocus-pocus equipment designed to distort reality—"

"Wrongo, Moosebreath," she cried, and softened somewhat when he got the reference to Bullwinkle Moose and Rocky the Flying Squirrel from old television shows. "I'm not claiming what I do is real. I'm no Moses Weiss." She saw they didn't connect. "Moses Weiss really does talk to dead people. And it drove the poor man bonkers. I am happy to admit that I cook the books, make it believable enough to keep the audiences coming back. But… "

She leaned across the table and fixed him with an unwavering look.

"I trick the equipment, 'manage the readings,' warp the outcome to create the most entertaining effect. Weren't you listening to what I said before? The same instruments I use are used by scientists to document real phenomena. If there really is some—" She must have seen skepticism in his and Cotton's faces. "I'm not using the G word, ghost, okay. But some kind of … entity, spiritual phenomena, sentient being. What'd you call it — the Jabberwock? Doesn't matter what you call it, if there really is something there, this equipment will show us where and what it is."

"What's the point?" Cotton wanted to know. He rubbed his eyes to clear them, leaving them even more red than they already were. "So we find out there is … what? A spirit? A poltergeist? Casper and all his significant others?" He stopped and barked out a sardonic laugh. "How come all ghosts are *white*? Did you ever wonder about that?"

Jolene looked mildly uncomfortable, the way most white people looked when they were forced to actually *recognize* the skewed-white distortion of the world.

"I've noticed," Stuart said. "When my grandmother died, I wondered if she'd come back as a white ghost. That's when I decided all ghosts were white because if they were black you couldn't see them in the dark."

Cotton dragged the conversation back to the point.

"So we can demonstrate they're here — what good does that do? Maybe you weren't tracking with Stuart and me when I said I have spent two weeks trying to get people to believe there is something horribly wrong here, that thousands of people have vanished. And there's plenty of *evidence*, hard, factual, you-can-hold-it-in-your-hand evidence to *prove* that, but—"

"What if it's not just *you* saying the sky is falling. What if there are fifty, a hundred, a *thousand* Chicken Littles?"

"I don't get what—" Stuart said.

"If I get the kind of real readings that I believe I'll get — not fraudulent, cooking-the-books, but *real* — can you imagine the explosion it'll cause when I tell this whole story on my show? With indisputable, scientific proof and a whole county full of empty houses? The road to Nowhere County will be clogged with cars all the way to Lexington. You'll be tripping over nut-bag ghost-crazies and real scientists and lookie-loos and everything in between."

"What good will—?" Cotton began.

"They'll see. Don't you get it, they'll *see*. They may be coming here looking for ghosts, but when they get here they'll notice that, oh by the way, *a whole county full of people really is missing*."

"But they'll forget—"

"You sure about that? Are you *sure* this Jabberwock thing can wipe the minds of dozens, hundreds, maybe thousands of people?"

She had a point. In truth, they didn't have any idea what the Jabberwock thing could or could not do. Just how powerful was it?

It was certainly worth a try to find out.

Chapter Eight

MALACHI LOOKED like Sam had slapped him. He didn't literally stagger backward a step, but she could see him do it psychologically, could see him withdraw from information he flat out did not want to know. Who could blame him?

Sam had always felt sorry for Malachi because she believed, genuinely believed, that he was cut from an entirely different cloth than the other members of his murderous crime family. He wasn't like his mother and brothers. As far as she knew, there was a short period of time after high school when Malachi had joined in with the others in the family business. She wasn't sure about the particulars because she was pregnant with Rusty, and had way bigger fish to fry than wondering about a former classmate's criminal activity. By the time Sam got her head above water again, with a goal in life, a toddler to raise and a determination to make something of herself, Malachi seemed to have been bitten by the same bug. He'd left Nower County for the military, and for the next decade he was only back intermittently. She only found out that he'd been home after he had left. It was a stroke of coincidence that he'd been home on leave when his brother got the infected spider bite. Otherwise, Sam wouldn't have seen Malachi at all since graduation more than a decade ago.

Seeing him now reacting to her words confirmed for her what she had always believed — that Malachi had no idea what his mother was capable of doing.

Though she and Charlie had not spoken about it last night as they were seeing to Liam … to his body … Sam suspected Charlie shared her fear that the reason Malachi had not shown up at the meeting he'd promised to attend with them, the reason he hadn't made his "little speech" that Charlie had ended up making for him, was because he knew what his mother and brothers intended to do. And either he wanted no part of it, and so he stayed away, or he was in cahoots with them and his absence was part of Viola's plan to take over the county.

Now, seeing the look on his face when she accused his mother of killing Liam, it was clear to Sam that Malachi had not been privy to his mother's plan to overthrow the law enforcement of the county and install herself as the new dictator. He'd had no idea she'd planned to kill Liam. In fact, Sam saw denial in his eyes, a pulling back, a refusal to believe his mother — even given what he had seen her do in the past — could be heartless, *soul-less* enough to murder poor Liam Montgomery in cold blood.

"Why … what makes you think …?"

Sam laid it out in simple statements. It was clear Viola had the whole thing planned out in advance — had orchestrated "disturbances" that suddenly broke out all over the room at the same time while she and her sons took up strategic positions on the stage.

"I saw her in the back of the room with your brothers," Charlie said. "And the next thing I knew, the meeting broke out in arguments — everywhere at once — bickering that was heating up toward violence."

Sam continued her description of what happened.

"People started pulling weapons, the place was seconds away from something like a shootout and Liam leapt off the stage and waded into the crowd to calm things down."

"Then there was a gunshot, a single gunshot," Charlie said.

"And Liam was lying on the floor, bleeding to death." Sam's voice was suddenly tear-clotted.

"So you didn't see my mother shoot—?"

"I didn't have to see it!" Sam was grateful for the anger that boiled up in her belly. It gave her the strength to push through all she had to say. "She was on the stage, just appeared there as soon as Liam jumped into the crowd. It wasn't random, chance. She didn't just happen to be nearby. She and your brothers were positioned there — like soldiers — spaced out across the front of the stage with weapons drawn."

"Getting the drop on everyone," Charlie said. "I saw her and the others when they came in and your mother was *not* packing a 30-06 rifle! I'd have noticed! Which means she had it all planned out in advance, had weapons stashed somewhere for her to grab when she needed them."

"I don't know if anybody actually saw who did the shooting," Sam said. "If anybody did, they kept what they saw to themselves because nobody came forward. It was so confused and happened so fast."

"But you think my mother—"

"Liam was shot in the back, Malachi." Sam's words rode a sob out of her throat. "And the only person standing *behind* him was—"

"My mother," he finished for her.

She watched emotions play across his face in the silence that followed.

"She planned the whole thing," he said simply.

"It's easy to see *now* that it was orchestrated like a ballet. One minute she and your brothers are in the back of the room standing against the wall. Then the fights break out and bada boom, bada bing, she's on the stage … *with a deer rifle!*"

"She planned it, *all of it,*" Malachi said.

Sam couldn't determine the exact emotion she heard in the words, and maybe there was no emotion at all. None he would allow to come through.

"She planned to take over and …" There was only the hint of a hesitation before he went on, "… and she *planned to kill Liam*. Of course she did. He stood between her … He was the only legitimate authority that stood between her and her own little country."

"There's no way to prove it," Charlie said. "In a normal world, with amenities like 911 and the Kentucky State Police, autopsies and ballistics — somebody would be able to match the bullet in Liam's back to—"

"But it's not a normal world in Nowhere County, and …" Sam heard her own thoughts coming out in her words, spoke it before she even understood the implications, "… and I don't think it ever will be again unless *we* do something. Who else is doing anything to try to figure this out? If not us, who?"

"It's more than that," Charlie said, and both of them turned to look at her. "It's not just that we're the only ones trying to understand. It's — I think it … the Jabberwock is …" Now, it was clear Charlie didn't want to continue. But she pushed through it. "I think maybe the … thing … is trying to … it's *talking* to me."

That was a conversation stopper. There was a beat of

absolute silence. Another. And then each of them drew in a breath, eager to ask/say/speak—

But none of them got the chance, because into their silence fell a voice from down the hall, the voice of her son, Rusty.

"Mom, come quick. Something's wrong with E.J."

Chapter Nine

As SOON AS she'd convinced Cotton and Stuart to go along, Jolene started laying her plans.

"We could set up this equipment anywhere, but I want to test my father's house. There is *something* there. I know it. I felt it."

"Something," Stuart said. "Yeah, I'll bet there's definitely *something*."

There wasn't a shred of disbelief on Cotton's face either. And that was a first. The people with whom she came in contact in her line of work were always somewhere along a scale from "you are a crazy woman or a liar" all the way to "ask my dead Uncle Hurl where he put the safety deposit box key." But nobody just took the existence of spirits without a shred of argument or disbelief the way Stuart McClintock and Cotton Jackson did. That in itself was spooky because their lack of disbelief had nothing to do with faith in her or in her equipment. They *knew* she wasn't making stuff up. And that gave her a genuine case of the willies.

They all loaded into her van. The sky had grown even

more overcast while they talked and now hung in a gray, brooding canopy above their heads. During the short trip from Persimmon Ridge to her father's house in the Middle of Nowhere she began an explanation of the equipment she'd be using and how it worked, starting with the Gauss-Master EMF meter.

"It has probes, sensors that measure electromagnetic fields. A really good probe doesn't disturb the field, and has to prevent coupling and reflection to get precise results. There are two main types of EMF measurements: broadband and frequency-selective measurements. Broadband uses a probe that senses any electromagnetic signal across a wide range of frequencies — mine has three independent diode detectors. Frequency-selective measurements use a field antenna or spectrum analyzer to monitor the frequency range."

She paused when no one spoke, then continued proudly, "You can get EMF probes that respond to fields only on one axis, but *mine* is triaxial, showing a field in three different directions at once."

When she paused again, Cotton spoke from the backseat.

"Supercalifragilisticexpialidocious."

She made eye contact with him in the rearview mirror. "What?"

"Or you can say it backwards," Stuart said from beside her in the front of the van, "which is docious, ali, expi, istic, fragi, cali, repus."

"And your point?"

"Either one of them makes as much sense as what you're saying," Cotton said. "And I used to be a mathematics teacher."

"Save the explanations for the folks who tune in to your show and buy enough toothpaste or running shoes or car insurance to keep the advertisers happy," Stuart said. "Just set it up, turn it on and we'll see if it has anything to report."

She sighed. "Fine. But it's a bummer. This is the first time in my multifaceted career that there might actually be a paranormal presence to find, and there's nobody here to see that I didn't screw with the results to make it happen."

The moment they pulled into her father's driveway, Jolene began to feel cold all over. She'd have turned down the air conditioning, but it wasn't on.

"You guys feel—?"

"Cold?" Stuart responded. "Uh huh."

"Copy that," Cotton said from the backseat.

She couldn't keep the silly grin from creeping out onto her face or the excitement out of her voice.

"It's real. Nothing made up. This is such a rush!"

"Let's see if you're still thrilled when we get in there and the … presence wants us to leave," Stuart said.

The excitement drained away as she recalled how she had been violently expelled from the premises only a few hours before.

Opening the sliding side door of the van, she gestured toward what must have looked like a Rube Goldberg creation to the two men, and asked if they'd help her carry the various pieces of equipment into the house.

"Everything but that," she said, pointing to the machine stuck back behind the others. "It's a—" She caught herself. "It's a thingamabob that emits ultra high frequency sound waves. Higher than a dog whistle."

"What's it for?" Cotton asked.

"Bug spray for ghosts. Gets rid of them."

"Does it work?"

"How would I know? I've never used it on a real ghost."

Cotton and Stuart got the machinery out of the van, set it on the rolling cart, and pushed it up the sidewalk and into the house. She crossed the yard behind them, and the closer she got to the house, the more aware she was that whatever it was that now … occupied … the residence was not happy to see her. Even after they'd hauled everything into the living room, she left the door open because the stuffiness in the air seemed to grow more uncomfortable by the minute. The open door wouldn't help but it was all she could do.

"Well would ya look at this!" Cotton stepped up to the canvas in the living room, staring in admiration at the map that took up almost the whole wall.

"Your father drew this?" Stuart asked her and she nodded.

"All those years as a mail carrier, probably wasn't anybody in the county knew it better than he did," Cotton said.

"Good to see a map of the county that actually has the name on it," Stuart said, and when they both looked at him, he continued. "You haven't noticed?" They shook their heads.

He reached into his suit coat pocket and took out a map. He said he'd gotten it at the convenience store on the way into Nower County, that it had taken ten minutes to re-fold it properly after he'd opened it, sitting in front of the gigantic hole blasted in the asphalt. He opened the map again and held it up awkwardly for them to see.

"Nower County's not there," he said, pointing to the space between Beaufort and Drayton and Crawford counties. "Well, the *place* is there, but the name isn't. And this is the official map of Kentucky, that became effective" — he searched around on the legend page until he found it — "on June 1, 1995."

"Nower County isn't on the map." There was fear-tinged awe in Cotton's voice.

"You think that has anything to do with what's going on here?" Jolene asked.

"Yeah." His voice was soft. "But I don't know if it's cause or effect."

She watched him try to shake off the gloom that had settled around all of them, to no effect. It was a heavy, palpable presence, unshakeable.

"Set this stuff up and let's see what it says," Stuart said, and even the guy built like a professional wrestler looked around apprehensively. "So we can get out of here."

Chapter Ten

IT WAS INSTANTLY clear that E.J. was having a seizure. What wasn't at all clear was why.

Sam and the others raced down the hallway to find E.J. in the bed, hooked up to the IV lines, his back rigid and his eyes rolled back. He was convulsing violently. Sam scrambled to remember words on a page in a textbook, describing a phenomenon she never expected to see up close and personal. And she'd never have dreamed she would be responsible for figuring it all out and doing the right thing in response.

A seizure was an electrical storm in the brain, a sudden burst of electrical activity. E.J. was suffering a grand mal seizure. Rusty was trying to restrain his heaving body.

"Let him go," Sam told her son. To Malachi, she said, "Help me roll him over onto his side, to keep his airway clear."

Malachi stepped forward and the two rolled E.J. onto his side, gently holding his jerking body in place. Sam looked at her watch, then realized the absurdity of the action. You were supposed to time the duration of a seizure so you could report it to the attending physician. *She* was the only physician, attending or otherwise.

Gratefully, the seizure subsided in a couple of minutes and E.J. regained consciousness. He was disoriented, but seemed otherwise unharmed. Looking at all the people gathered around his bed, he managed to whisper, "Who called this meeting?" and tried to grin. "I didn't get the memo."

But the seizure had banged his injured leg around and Sam knew it was likely screaming in pain. She glanced at the clock. He wasn't due for more pain medication — more of Malachi's contraband oxycontin — for another half hour, but she pulled the bottle out of the pocket of her white lab coat, popped a couple of pills into her hand and held E.J.'s head while he washed them down with a cup of water.

She eased him back down on the hospital bed Malachi had scrounged for him and they all made inane conversation as he got less and less coherent. He was soon asleep.

It wasn't until E.J. was resting comfortably again that Sam's hands began to shake. Malachi noticed, but said nothing. Just stepped quietly up to her and put his arm around her shoulders. She wanted so badly to turn into his embrace, throw her arms around him and burst into tears. She didn't, couldn't. If she let go of her grip on her emotions, relaxed, she would totally fall apart. And right now, as pitiful and ineffectual as she was, she was still the only person in the whole county with any medical training at all. E.J. needed her to hold it together.

"I've done … everything I can," she said, and was surprised that her voice wasn't shaking in rhythm with her hands. "Let's let him rest."

The puppy feeding was complete so Rusty and Merrie went out into the waiting room with Merrie pleading,

"Again, again! Read it again," clutching her battered copy of *Where the Wild Things Are* to her chest. Raylynn took up the post at E.J.'s bedside.

"He's alright now, isn't he?" she asked. "The seizure didn't hurt him, I mean — did it?"

The concern on her face, the fear in her voice, wasn't lost on Sam and she could see the others picked up on it, too. If they hadn't already figured it out, they knew now how the teenage girl felt about E.J.

"The seizure did no damage," Sam said, delicately tiptoeing around saying "he's fine" because he wasn't.

"Can we …?" Malachi had been standing by the door, unnoticed. "I think we still have things to talk about."

Sam nodded. Charlie met their eyes. "Give me a minute to take Merrie to the bathroom or she'll sit listening to Rusty read the story until she pees her pants."

Sam and Malachi went together into the breakroom, and Sam dutifully began to make coffee — mostly so she could keep her back turned to Malachi.

"I was watching you with E.J. We're all lucky to have you here."

She flat out could not do that.

With her back still turned to him, she cried out, "Malachi Tackett, if you ever say anything like that again, I will … I will …" She managed to stifle a sob, sensed his movement toward her and held up a restraining hand without turning. "Don't. Just don't. I am hanging on by my cuticles here and I …"

"I get it," he said. "Message received. I'm good."

And it was like Malachi'd been a stove with heat pulsing off it and he'd reached up and turned off the flame. He did something — maybe it was a thing he'd learned in the military, not in military training but a thing he had learned being a soldier, in combat, having to keep his own focus while the world was falling apart around him. He just pulled back behind some kind of barrier, a self-made wall, and operated from beyond it — where there was no emotional attachment to what was going on in the world around him.

Oh, how Sam wished he could teach her that trick.

Charlie came into the room.

"The 'wild things' are Merrie's spirit animals," she said. She looked at Sam. "Is Rusty alright with all this?"

"He's a tough kid."

"He's a *good* kid. You must be very proud of him."

Sam steeled herself, grabbed hold of every ounce of emotional strength she had, waiting … hoping Malachi wouldn't …

And he didn't. Malachi said nothing. And if he had … if he'd added praise for her son to the "you're doing a good job" remark, Sam would have completely lost it. He didn't. She didn't. And the moment passed.

"Let's make sure we're all singing from the same sheet of music," Malachi said, not looking at either of them as Sam set cups of coffee in front of them on the table. "I know that my mother is … I know she killed Liam." He spoke with no more emotion than the recorded message on an answering machine telling you to leave your phone number after the beep. She knew he was down deep in himself, launching the words up into the world from some-place cold and dark. "She *murdered* Liam." He took a breath. "He's not … the first man she's killed. And … there's not a thing we can do about it."

Sam wasn't expecting that part, but apparently Charlie was because she added, "So there's no sense in trying."

They both were right, of course. There was no way to prove what they knew to be true and nothing to be done about it if they could. Until … unless …

"The only thing we can do about Liam, and the only thing we can do to help E.J. …"

"And the only way we can manage not to vanish ourselves is to figure out what's happening and find a way to stop it, and the only way to do *that* is for everybody to come clean." Malachi turned to Charlie. "So what's this about the Jabberwock trying to communicate with you? How? And what's it saying?"

"The how is by … what's it called … ghost writing."

Sam wasn't tracking.

"When words appear and you didn't put them there." It was clear she did not want to go on. "Yesterday … there were words written in chalk on the blackboard in my mother's kitchen. I thought at the time they were in my"— a heartbeat pause that spoke volumes — "*husband's* hand-writing, but I convinced myself that I had done it myself and just didn't remember."

Charlie's husband.

The three of them had been up to their necks in all things Jabberwock for the past two weeks and there hadn't been a lot of emotional capital left over to spend on catching up on each other's lives. But in snatches of time here and there, the girls had tried. Sam had shared the short list of the near-misses in her singularly unimpressive love life since high school — including the pilot of the Stat-Flight helicopter from the University of Kentucky Medical Center who'd actually tried to seduce her while they were in the air.

Sam didn't have to share what'd happened to Jimbo Mattingly, her "steady" boyfriend all through school, though their relationship had blinked on and off like a Joe's Beer Joint sign their senior year. Everyone knew what'd happened to Jimbo. He'd died a hero three weeks after graduation when he'd saved the life of the son of

Steven Beshear, the state attorney general, after a fiery crash on the interstate. Four-year-old Andy Beshear had escaped uninjured; Jimbo had died of third-degree burns the next day.

Charlie had never shared what had happened to her husband and Sam had never asked. Watching Charlie's face now, it was obvious she was reluctant to put down a drawbridge across that moat, but she had no choice.

"I didn't say anything about it yesterday because if I had, then that would have opened up a subject I didn't want to talk about. A painful subject. My husband … his name is Stuart …"

And she had to pause after that to get her emotions in check before she could continue. It couldn't have been more plain if a red sign had started flashing on Charlie's forehead. She loved her husband but things were *not* going well between them.

"Stuart and I are … separated. It's not a pretty story but I am still willing to share it with you if you're interested. Right now, though, it's not the point. The point is that … I think he, at least I *thought* he … but there's no way it could possibly …"

"How about we agree right here and now that nothing is off the table on the weirdness scale," Malachi said. "We have to stop self-editing, assuming that what we saw or thought or felt was too bizarre to be real. In this Looney Tune world, nothing's impossible."

Charlie took a breath. "Okay, I don't believe now that I just wrote on the chalkboard and then didn't remember I'd done it. Besides, the words were not in my handwriting. They were in Stuart's."

"What did he say?"

"'Where are you?'"

There was silence.

"Which … would be a reasonable thing to ask … if you were looking for somebody," Sam said.

"When I saw the words, I was so shocked that I … I picked up the piece of chalk and wrote the first thing that came into my head: 'I'm trapped. It won't let me go.' Then I felt spectacularly foolish and erased all of it."

"Boy, oh boy, oh boy," Sam said, "does *this* open up a can of worms."

"There are more worms than you know," Charlie said. "Last night, I … when I got home, I went into the kitchen and — it was just an impulse — I wrote 'I want to go home!' on the blackboard."

She stopped. Sam absolutely did not want to know what happened next, but Malachi did, "And then …?"

"Words appeared under what I'd written. Not all of it at once — one letter at a time … like I was watching some-body write them."

"Stuart?"

"Absolutely *not* Stuart. Not his handwriting, not even in cursive. Block letters, all caps. The chalk marks looked like … somebody was pressing down hard."

"What did the words say?"

"'No. Stay here and play with me.'"

The room went dead silent.

Sam finally found her voice. "But *who* …?" Malachi just looked at her and she answered her own question. "The Jabberwock."

"It's all a game." Malachi's voice was equal parts dismay and wonder. "Some stupid *game!*"

"That doesn't make any sense," Charlie cried, then held up her hand before Malachi could admonish her that sense was no longer sense. "I know, I know—" Then she suddenly looked even more horrified. "The missing people, the ones who vanished — it took them to play a game?"

"Why them?" Sam asked. "Abner, Roscoe, Harry — why *those people*?"

"Random," Malachi said. "Luck of the draw. Spin the bottle."

"Let me get this straight … you think the Jabberwock came here and imprisoned the county so he could randomly grab people to play some kind of *game?* Is that what you're saying?"

"You got a better explanation?"

"But … what's the game?" Sam felt her throat tighten as she said it.

"Better question — what are *the rules*?" Malachi said. "Because we *have to* win!"

Chapter Eleven

STUART WATCHED Jolene move with practiced ease setting up equipment and he knew it wasn't his imagination that the longer they remained in the house, the more the sense of unwelcome grew. He seemed to be having trouble breathing, like there wasn't quite enough oxygen in the air. He couldn't tell if the others felt the same way. Cotton's shoulders were hunched, like he was hunkering down for a blow. On Jolene's face was a mixture of fear and excitement. He suspected that each of them was drawing strength from the presence of the others, that their experience would have been infinitely worse if they had come to the house alone.

Cotton was fascinated by the map, which gave him something to focus on to take his mind off the growing ... oppression in the room. Even Stuart could tell the map was something truly amazing. The detail was stunning. Clearly it had taken Jolene's father years to create it.

"There's Sharptop Mountain," Cotton said to himself, tracing a line with his finger across the map to an icon that indicated Sawmill Hollow. "I never realized it was that close to Sawmill." He looked at Stuart. "Mountain roads are like a mound of spaghetti, winding around wherever a creek has made a path through the hollows. Even if you've lived here your whole life, you kind of lose track of where things are — as the crow flies — in relation to other things."

Stuart noticed a pile of multicolored stickpins in a box and thought of the blackboard in Charlie's mother's kitchen, how he'd written on it and Charlie had responded. She had responded. She *had*. It wasn't his imagination.

Without thinking it through, he picked up a handful of stickpins, selecting only the black ones, and began sticking them into the map. Starting on the left, he placed a pin on the "a," the "r" and the "e" in the words "C**A**rson Sp**R**ings Lan**E**." Moving right, he placed a pin in the "y" and the "o" in the words Wile**Y** R**O**ad.

Cotton took note of what he was doing but said nothing, just watched. When he was finished, Cotton asked, "Think it'll work, do you?"

Stuart wanted to believe it was possible. "No."

"It's showtime," Jolene announced, pushing a strand of hair that kept falling in her eyes back behind her ear. "You guys ready for me to flip the switches?"

As if in response to her question, there was a low rumble from outside. Thunder. Just thunder. There was a storm building. Nothing sinister about that. But Stuart saw the other two look around as if they didn't like the grumbling sound any more than he did.

"You don't have to do anything ... say anything?" Cotton asked.

She chuckled. "If we were on the air, I'd have all manner of things to say, adjustments to make to the equipment, while I told you what to expect the meters to show. What the readings would be in a "normal" room and what *might* … not likely but *might* show in the event we had company."

She suddenly seemed nervous and turned back to the equipment.

"This may be the first time I've ever used this stuff in an effort to see what *really is* in a room."

He watched her move from one piece of equipment to another flipping switches. She didn't even have to turn it all on before company showed up.

PETE RUTHERFORD STOPPED at his back door and looked at his watch, then looked at the thermometer that hung on the wall beside the screen.

"Seventy-six degrees," he told Dog, who looked from the thermometer to Pete and back at the thermometer, just like he knew what Pete was saying. "Right on schedule. It's ten o'clock and it's seventy-six degrees. Every day since J-Day …" He let it go. He wasn't telling Dog nothing the dog didn't already know.

In the bright sunshine, he squinted up from beneath his bushy eyebrows at the pristine sky and said in mock surprise, "And would you look at that. Why … there's not a single cloud. Imagine that."

He shook his head as he leaned over to remove the leash from Dog's collar. The dog sat still while he did it. They had an agreement, him and the dog. The dog would pretend that he couldn't get out of the leash, and therefore it was a good idea to put it on him when they went for a walk, and Pete would pretend he didn't know the dog could wiggle free from the thing in a New York minute.

"Ain't seen a cloud in the sky in so long I'm beginning to forget what one looks like." Dog understood. He listened with equal interest in the evenings when the dark blue of the sky turned black after the sun finally set out there on the flat, if indeed, there was an out there … and a real sun. Then Pete railed against the random lights — equal size and shape and none of them twinkled — that now occupied the slice of sky above the hollow, replacing the constellations, the Big Dipper, Cassiopeia and all the others that were Pete's friends. Gone.

"It's all been gobbled up by the dadgum Jabberwock," he told Dog, said it defiant-like. If the Jabberwock thought he was gonna cow Pete Rutherford with a fake sky and thermostat temperatures, he had one or two more thinks coming. Might be Pete would disappear — like Abner and Reece Tibbits and Harry Tungate. Go poof in a puff of smoke or whatever form it took when you was "gobbled up by the Jabberwock." If that was the case, fine by Pete. Wasn't no way he was gonna see another Christmas anyway — even if he followed every one of Sam Sheridan's live-until-Christmas rules — so wasn't no never mind to him one way or the other.

He paused, allowed himself to think the thought that'd been buzzing around the outsides of his mind for a right smart while now. The big C … it'd been in remission long's he was taking them chemotherapy drugs in Carlisle twice a week. But soon's he quit going there for treatments …

He'd first noticed it a week after J-Day. The ache deep in his belly was back. He ignored it, told himself, and Dog — he'd took to telling that little animal everything — that it was just something he'd eaten disagreed with him. That he'd be fine after a strong dose of that nasty pink stuff — Pepto-Bismol. 'Cept he wasn't fine. The ache remained. He kinda pictured it in his mind like a little bitty piece of charcoal, size of a marble deep in his belly. A cherry red piece of charcoal, like something fell out past the grate from a fire when you was banking it in the wintertime.

That marble … it was getting bigger. Oh, not growing up big as a tennis ball overnight or nothing like that. But it was growing. The thing, the … the cancer was growing. Them treatments had kept it the same size, didn't get rid of it or nothing magical as that, but they held it at bay, one little dandelion in the grass. Now, wasn't nothing keeping it from taking over the whole yard, and that's what it'd do. Them oncologists said it'd metastasize, like blowing on the puffball on the top of the dandelion, it'd fly out into his bloodstream and plant little seeds everywhere.

Might be going poof in a puff of smoke, courtesy of the Jabberwock'd be an easier way to go than all them little fires that was at that moment lighting up all over him.

No, that wasn't the way of it. If Pete Rutherford was gonna step outta this world, he'd do it natural-like, not absorbed by some sparkly mirage thing.

"Bring it!" he called out to the phenomenon that was everywhere and nowhere, that had locked up a couple thousand people and was systematically … what? Digesting them? "Go on, take your best shot."

Nothing happened. Least not yet.

Pete did wonder, though, if when the Jabberwock come for him at last if it'd leave Dog be. He hoped so. That old dog deserved a better end to his life than the one the Jabberwock had in store for the Nowhere people.

Chapter Twelve

STUART AND JOLENE felt it the same time Cotton did. The heavy atmosphere in the room got suddenly heavier — felt like the room had too much in it, too many people, too many ... somethings. It felt like they were jammed into a phone booth in London, all three of them at the same time. Not a spacious British phone booth, a Manhattan phone booth that'd be a tight squeeze for Superman all by himself.

Jolene was tinkering with some doodad or another and she stopped, her hand poised over a knob and looked fearfully at Cotton and Stuart.

They all sensed it.

Then the room started to get dark. No, that wasn't possible. It was overcast, but it was still *morning* outside. It didn't matter where the sun happened to be in the sky, inside Pete Rutherford's house in the Middle of Nowhere, the living room began to grow darker by the second.

They exchanged a look, horror registering with them all at the same time — the only way what was happening, the scary supernatural things going on around them, could conceivably get worse was … duh, if they were in the dark.

It came for them quickly, a great, black presence whose breath smelled of sulphur.

Stuart took a couple of steps and grabbed Jolene's arm, nodded toward Pete, who hurried across the room to them and grabbed Jolene's other hand as the lights went totally out.

Dark.

It was a kind of dark that Jolene and Stuart had likely never experienced. Cotton had. He'd spent a miserable couple of months as a young man working in a coal mine and the absolute, impenetrable blackness of that dark was intimidating by its very nature. This darkness felt like that.

There was a sudden flare of light. Jolene had pulled out a lighter and stroked the striker wheel. The three of them appeared in the flickering light, their faces masks of the fear and confusion. Then their eyes were drawn to the flame itself. In stunned horror, they watched the flame begin to shrink. It grew smaller and smaller until it was a pinprick of flickering light, a tiny flame between the metal prongs of the lighter.

But it didn't go out entirely.

Somehow that was worse — a tiny pinprick of flickering flame, making shadows dance on the walls around them.

An indicator light on one of the machines came on, turned instantly green and then began to flash red. Before Jolene could turn to the machine, something appeared in the far corner of the room.

An apparition. A white blob of protoplasm … something. Nothing. No, *some*thing.

The ceiling began to turn red, an odd shade of dark red, the color of …

Blood began to drip from the ceiling in big globs that made sounds, splats like raindrops, on the floor.

"It's not real." Jolene's voice was airless. "Hallucination, something. Not really happening."

A man's face appeared in the whiteness in the far corner.

A white blob appeared in the other corner, where an identical face appeared.

It wasn't the same face, or even a mirror image of it. There were two *almost-identical* faces staring out into the room. One of them had blind eyes and the face from which the eyes stared sightlessly was expressionless, slack. The other's eyes were searching frantically, the face a mask of fear and desperation.

And the blood drip, drip, dripped from the ceiling.

"It's Roscoe and Harry," Cotton gasped. "The Tungate brothers."

The blank stare left the blind eyes then — Roscoe Tungate, Cotton thought. The one whose eyes were alive and searching was Roscoe. Harry's eyes trained on Cotton, fixed him with a hostile stare. The stare sparked with emotion, a look like a flashing sword, rage and anger blazing in the eye sockets like the sparks off a welding torch.

"You don't belong here!"

The voice wasn't Cotton's imagination. The others heard it, too. But it was neither Harry nor Roscoe's voice. Cotton had gone fishing with the two of them several times, knew them well enough to tell them apart, which was something of an accomplishment with the Tungates. In fact, the voice didn't really sound like anybody's voice, any human's. There was no inflection in it at all. Harry's face looked enraged, Roscoe still didn't appear to notice anything, was frantically looking for something. But the voice that spoke in the room was almost soothing.

No, not soothing. Simple.

Childlike.

"I don't want to play with you," the voice said. "Go away."

Then the faces began to expand, grew bigger than the walls of the room around them, which was impossible but that's what they did. The white faces loomed over them, getting closer and closer. Jolene and Cotton began to move backward but Stuart held their hands firm, and wouldn't let them budge.

"What have you done with them?" Stuart called out, and for all his standing firm, there was an unmistakable quiver in his voice. He must have felt it, firmed it up, because there was no tremor in his voice when he spoke again. "Let them go!"

There was an explosion of sound that rattled the fillings in Cotton's teeth, that slapped him backward with the percussion of an exploding stick of dynamite, that got inside his head somehow and echoed off the inside walls of his skull, the echoes not getting softer, as echoes did, but getting louder with every repetition, until the word was repeated again and again, words on top of words, a cacophony of sound, all speaking the same word.

"Nooooooo!"

Pete never locked his doors. Nobody in Nowhere County did.

He opened the back screen, turned the knob and shoved the back door inward and stepped through it into the kitchen, letting the screen bang shut behind him. He left Dog on the back porch. The dog's mangy coat had so little identifiable fur it was amazing he was able to shed even a single hair of it, but in truth there was a slathering of black and gray hairs anywhere the animal touched so he was not allowed into the house on the furniture.

The animal usually curled up in a ball on the mat right in front of the door, so he'd be alerted if Pete decided he wanted to go somewhere. At some point, Dog had decided Pete was his human, and he appeared to be determined never to be more than three feet from Pete's side.

He didn't curl up on the mat today, though. He glared through the screen door into the kitchen and began to growl, a low, angry growl.

Pete froze.

Images from last night's county meeting flashed instantly into his mind. Liam Montgomery was dead, shot down in a roomful of people and Pete'd lay odds not a single one of them saw who pulled the trigger. It wasn't hard to figure out the most likely suspect, given that Viola Tackett had swooped in like a Blackhawk helicopter looking for wounded, and in less than a minute took over the county lock, stock and barrel.

She would be the law in Nowhere County from now on. Which meant, of course, that there would be no law at all in the county, just the foxes watching the henhouse. Wouldn't be anarchy — but it would be a dictatorship, and he doubted Viola Tackett was planning on being a benevolent dictator.

So if … say somebody broke into Pete's house and wanted to steal — what? Shoot, he didn't own a single thing anybody would want — not even some big nice television. Even if he'd had one, there hadn't been any reception since J-Day so why would anybody want it? Still, the dog was growling at something, most likely, from the sound of it, some*one*. And whatever happened between Pete and the intruder in the next few minutes would fall to Viola Tackett to judge the lawfulness or unlawfulness thereof.

That was not comforting.

"Anybody here?" he called out, and was impressed his voice wasn't shaking. "You're welcome to anything I got, but I'd appreciate it if you'd leave now 'cause my dog is not a happy camper."

Nothing but silence, full and heavy, came back to him from his words.

Dog continued to growl, a sound unlike any Pete had ever heard the dog make, not that he'd lay claim to knowing the subtle difference in dog language. His ears were laid back flat on his head, his eyes were open wide, the hair on his shoulders — his hackles — was standing on end and his teeth were bared in a vicious snarl.

Whoever was in the house would do well to exit by the front door because wasn't no telling what that dog might do to whoever he caught. From the look of him, he wasn't likely to jump up for an ear rub or roll over on his back for a belly rub.

"Whoever you are — you need to book it out of here. My dog looks in the mood to rip your leg off."

Shouldn't have said that. If the guy had a gun, he might shoot Dog and the thought of something bad happening to the animal planted a stab of fear in Pete's gut.

Nobody answered. Dog continued to growl.

Wasn't nothing for it but to go on in the house and make nice with whoever it was who'd decided to rob an old man who didn't have nothing, a man who lived — literally, as it turned out — in the Middle of Nowhere.

Pete advanced slowly across the kitchen, straining to

hear any sound of movement from the house. He heard nothing.

But the nothing was a funny kind of nothing. It was the kind of nothing that was like the perfect temperature and the blue sky and the phony stars. It wasn't natural, normal. It was oppressive, heavy silence, like he'd walked into King Tut's tomb and the dude in the crypt was not happy about it.

He had a sudden desire to call out, "Olly olly oxen free!" A kid's game. Why had a thing like that popped into his head?

Advancing into the living room, the silence got more oppressive with every step, and outside on the porch, Dog didn't let up on his ominous growl.

It took considerable effort to force himself to search the house, but there was nothing else for it. Dog was growling at something, but after a thorough inspection of every room — under beds and in closets included — Pete could find nobody.

Against his hard and fast rule, Pete went back to the door and opened it to allow Dog into the house, follow him to see what he was growling at. But the dog wouldn't set foot through the door. Pete called, cajoled, even went to the fridge and got out a piece of the last chicken Pete had cooked on the grill.

Zip.

The dog could not be enticed to come into the house. Neither did he stop growling.

This was exceedingly weird.

Pete decided to search the house again, not looking for anybody this time but for some indication, any indication at all, that somebody had trespassed on his abode, looking for anything out of place that would indicate somebody'd been here.

He found what he was looking for in the living room.

He might not even have noticed it if he hadn't stopped in front of the map to think, figure out what he ought to—

There were stickpins in the map. Stickpins Pete hadn't put there.

Chapter Thirteen

AND THEN IT WAS GONE.

Everything.

The artificial darkness, the sense of oppression, the white blobs of protoplasm, the bloody ceiling — everything disappeared in the blink of an eye.

Jolene, Cotton and Stuart stood in the living room of Pete Rutherford's house, the only indication of their shared experience the lighter in Jolene's hand. She was holding it out in front of her with the flame turned up to its full two-inch height. Her hand began to tremble and she let go of the wheel and the flame when out.

Then Stuart let out the breath he hadn't even realized he'd been holding. The others did the same thing, at the same time — all noticed it, and managed to summon a communal sense of the humorousness of the act and they all visibly relaxed.

"Sooooo," Stuart said, surprised at the tremor in his voice. "Am I the only one who just had an out-of-body experience complete with visuals?"

"That'd be a no," Cotton said, his voice no more firm than Stuart's.

"And I wasn't smoking *nothing!*" Jolene's voice was as trembly as her hand. Then she turned and rushed to her equipment, looking at dials and measurements, meters and gadgetry.

"The ceiling did bleed, right?" Cotton said.

"Yup," Stuart said.

"And the Tungate brothers showed—"

"I heard you call the faces 'Tungate,'" Stuart said. "What—?"

"Roscoe and Harry Tungate, they're identical twins. Harry is a farmer who lives in Solomon Hollow and Roscoe is the butcher at Foodtown."

"So it wasn't the same face, two images?"

"Nope, two people. The one who appeared to be … the one who gave us the evil eye was Roscoe. Harry just looked—"

"Holy crap." Jolene's voice was breathy. "I never in a million years would have orchestrated something like this. It's too outrageous, too over-the-top. The electromagnetic field—"

"No mayonnaise words, remember," Cotton said and Jolene smiled like she knew what that meant. Stuart was clueless and they noticed.

"It's a thing Southerners … or maybe just Nowhere People say," Jolene said. "From some old story … I don't even know why. It just means speak in simple words."

"No words with more letters in them than 'mayonnaise,'" Cotton finished.

"Fine, no mayonnaise words. These instruments show a phenomenal psychic event. Like … say you're used to studying the results of firecrackers popping. Day in, day out, that's what you see — different firecracker events. But if you're really lucky, once every decade or so, you get to see a stick of dynamite." She stopped, took a breath. "This" — she made a gesture that included everything around them — "was what they dropped out of the Enola Gay on Hiroshima."

"So you're saying we didn't imagine what we saw."

"Yeah, that's what I'm saying. Can't write it off as group hysteria, a shared hallucination, something we cooked up in our heads that wasn't really reflected in an observable phenomenon in the real world."

"What we saw ... it was *real?*" Cotton asked.

"Define real?"

"Real!"

"The images we saw — the faces, the bleeding ceiling — they were *real images*." She turned to the equipment. "I've got measurements of them here. But there wasn't real blood."

"Meaning?"

"If any one of us had been willing to do so at the time, and I sure as Jackson wouldn't have volunteered, we could have stepped forward and touched the blood dripping down the walls. Blood we all could *see*. But if I'd touched it, there would have been no actual blood on my fingers."

"Okay, okay, let me get this straight in my head," Cotton said. "Some ... something is able to create images—"

"Not just images," Stuart added. "Feelings, too, and smells—"

"Think of it as a hologram ... on steroids. It looks real." She stopped. "The image of Princess Leia that Luke saw when he pushed the disc into R2D2. Like that. The image is *really there*. But the image itself isn't real."

"Okay, so ..."

"The readings on all these machines are recorded. There's a record of it all!"

Stuart stopped because he noticed that Cotton wasn't standing with him in front of Jolene's equipment. He had walked over to the map and was staring up at it.

"So is that real?" he asked and pointed to the stickpins in the map. Stuart had placed black stickpins on letters in the map. Now, there were red stickpins there, too.

The three exchanged a look, then Stuart picked up another handful of black stickpins — placed them at intervals across the map, spelling out his name.

"Now what?" Cotton said.

"Now we pack up my equipment and put it back in the van and then …"

"Then we wait for somebody on the other end of the stickpin telegraph to respond," Stuart said.

Once the equipment was loaded, they went into the living room and sat down on the floor to wait. One hour. Two. They didn't say much, each trying in their own way to wrap their minds around what was happening. Each considering their own personal "now what?"

Finally Stuart got to his feet.

"I think it's time to call this one. Apparently, the line's gone dead." He paused, then pushed forward with an effort. "And I have an idea."

"So do I," Cotton said.

"I have lots of ideas. Dozens. Hundreds." Jolene reached up her hand and Stuart pulled her to her feet. "But I don't know where to start."

Cotton nodded toward Stuart. "You got the ball, run with it."

"I think we ought to take the equipment out to Reece Tibbits's house," Stuart said.

"That was *one* of my ideas," Jolene said. "I'd be very

interested to know what kind of readings we'd get in a hundred-year-old house."

Cotton nodded.

"Sounds like a plan," he said, "but you don't need me to pull it off. I'm going to Lexington." He looked at Stuart. "Maybe you don't know this — Jolene does — but this isn't the first instance of 'vanishing people' in the county's history."

He told Stuart about a little town called Gideon beside a waterfall in a place called "Fearsome Hollow" that supposedly became a ghost town overnight about a century ago — just stories, a myth. Cotton said he'd considered the possibility of some connection in the very beginning, had gone out there, wandered around, found nothing.

"But we saw people, *identifiable people from Nowhere County who have vanished* — at least holograms of them. And that got me thinking. My wife was a history teacher, genealogy nut, did all kinda research. There's boxes full of it in our storage unit. I'm thinking now I'd like to see if she dug up anything about the people who lived in Gideon."

"Hate for you to miss the show, Cotton." Stuart turned toward Jolene. "If we're going to do this, let's get after it before I lose my nerve."

His voice was firm and that was good because *something* inside Stuart McClintock needed to be! The whole rest of his body was quaking like Jell-O. He was glad Jolene didn't appear to be a football fan and hadn't "recognized him." He just hoped she couldn't see how utterly terrified the big-shot football star was.

PETE STOOD STARING at the stickpins. Why in the name of common sense would somebody break into his house and leave without stealing anything? And technically, he couldn't say nobody *broke in* given that the door wasn't locked. But that was neither here nor there. Somebody had been in here and the only evidence of their presence was stickpins in his map.

Random stickpins.

That was something as nutty as the Jabberwock itself.

The Jabberwock.

Dog was still standing at the screen door, growling.

Pete felt a chill start down the back of his neck, felt like somebody'd poured ice water down his shirt collar and he could feel it sliding slowly along his back bone, dripping from one vertebrate to the next.

Maybe hadn't nobody been in his house. Least not nobody from here, some live human being walking around right now in Nowhere County. Maybe the somebody who'd put the stickpins …

And the more he looked at them … them stickpins wasn't random, neither. They was all lined up across the map, not in no straight line like blackbirds sitting on a clothesline. But close.

Didn't take but a minute to figure out. Them stickpins was each stuck into a letter of the alphabet in some word. If you started at the far left, the west side, and went across, the letters spelled out: "Are you there."

When he seen it, he took a step back, sucked in a gasp.

He looked around then, like maybe there was somebody in the room with him. Somebody maybe Dog could see but he couldn't.

Wasn't nobody there.

Dog was still growling.

Pete went to the box of stickpins sitting beside the map and picked up a handful. Sorting them out, he used only red stickpins.

Starting below the row of black stickpins on the map, he put red ones in letters of the alphabet, going from left to right, all the way to the Crawford County line on the east.

Then he stepped back, looked at what he had done — "Who are you?"

Dog suddenly shut up.

It was abrupt, like turning off a spigot.

Pete turned and went through the kitchen to the back door. He found the dog curled up in his usual place on the back porch rug, nodding off to sleep, like he didn't have a care in the world.

Whatever it was that had upset the dog wasn't upsetting him anymore. Whatever ... thing had been in the house was gone now.

Shaking his head, Pete went back into the living room. When he saw the map, he couldn't breathe. It felt like a wrecking ball had just slammed into his chest.

The original black stickpins that'd been in the map were gone. But there were new ones to take their place. Starting on the left side, the pins spelled out two words. A name: Stuart McClintock.

Chapter Fourteen

SHEPHERD CLAYTON'S mama had reamed him out good. She hadn't unloaded a come-to-Jesus like that on him since he was fifteen and him and Jim Bob Claywell got drunk, went joyriding on the McGintys' Farmall tractor and run it off into the creek. She'd laid him out for not staying home with Cody. She'd gone on and on about how his son needed him, and how he wasn't living up to his responsibilities as a father sitting in this old house day after day while others took care of his baby boy.

She'd said the same thing before, but she got on a roll this morning, said she wasn't gonna carry him over to him and Abby's place like she and the others had been doing, that he needed to stay where he was and look after his boy. So he'd took out walking. It was fifteen miles from his folks' house on Oldham Pike in Beaufort County to him and Abby's place at the end of the dirt road off Sawmill Lane in Nower County and it'd a took him all day to get there. He knew his mama wouldn't let him walk all that way and sure enough she come along after a while and give him a lift, but took up where she'd left off, flat out would not let it be. She said she and his daddy was real disappointed in him — and his daddy with MS and all. That hurt his feelings. She said his whole family was upset with him, particularly his sisters Clarice and Loretta, the ones that was taking care of Cody. They had they own kids to raise, his mama said, had plenty on their plates already 'thout him dumping his newborn on them and expecting them to look after him. Cody being so little and all it was a handful and he didn't have no right to palm it off on somebody else.

She kept at it, but he didn't say nothing. Wasn't no way to explain. She'd never understand the truth of it. Shep *was* home. *This* was his home, his and Abby's and Cody's. He was here with Abby and soon's things was made right, they'd all be here, him and Abby and Cody, all here in the house Abby'd come home to fix up the night before Cody'd been released from the hospital.

When Shep didn't never respond, his mama finally give up and left and he was powerful glad of it because with her jawing in his ear he couldn't hear Abby. Soon's he was alone in the house, he could hear her clear. In the beginning, it had been hard to pick her voice out of the whispers in the house. It'd got easier every day, until now it was just like she was sitting right here beside him, her talking in that voice that always reminded him of a little bird chirping — just like if they was back in life the way it used to be and she was sitting in the rocker nursing little Cody the way he'd dreamed of seeing her so many times he could close his eyes and make it real. In fact, in the last couple of days, he hadn't had to concentrate at all to hear her. But now, it wasn't like she was sitting beside him. It was more like she was *inside his head* and he didn't hear no "voice" at all.

In her not-voice that didn't sound like anybody at all, she told him about the world and what was going on in it that he didn't know about, things she knew about because … because she just knew, that's all.

He listened when she told him there was things he needed to do. At first, when she was still sitting beside him instead of talking inside his head, it was just conversation, suggestions like: *Shep, don't you think it'd be a good idea to see what it is that fella is up to, the one that come by here looking for his wife, Thelma?*

He'd allowed that they was lots of people looking for other people — everybody in Nower County was gone.

But she'd said that one fella was different — nosier than the rest.

Of course, she'd been right! He'd come back last night, brought that big guy with him. Shep didn't need Abby to tell him them fellas wasn't up to no good. Their kind never was. Abby told him the big one was married to a white woman so wasn't no telling what other evil he might be spawning. She told Shep what he needed to do about it and he'd do whatever she wanted because she was there inside him, directing him and—

"Yo Shep," someone said, and he liked to jumped out of his skin because wasn't nobody but him ever come by here, except his mama and she'd done come and gone for the day. He looked up at the door, which wasn't no proper door, of course, just a hole in the wall where there had been a door before the house … got old. He thought of it that way. The house got old after he come home to it and Abby wasn't there.

There was a man standing in the not-door, looking in at him where he sat in the lawn chair. He didn't know the man—

"It's me, Claude. I know I changed a lot but it pains me that my own kin don't know who I am no more."

Claude Letcher. Abby's oldest brother. And if he hadn't

told Shep who he was Shep wouldn't never have guessed it. Hadn't nobody in the family seen Claude in … what, ten years, maybe more'n that. He run off to the city when he was a teenager and got in all kinda trouble the family didn't like to talk about but Abby told him that he'd got to using drugs and selling them and other stuff just as bad.

Last he had heard of Claude was they'd locked him up somewhere in a mental hospital because they'd decided he wasn't sane enough to stand trial for the murder of his two roommates. Folks said he'd hacked them into little bitty pieces with a rusty hatchet when he was high on some drug or another, but apparently the drugs wasn't all. They'd said he had other mental problems, stuff wrong with him that didn't have nothing to do with drugs, but the drugs made it all worse.

He always had been odd and odd had over time turned into peculiar in a bad way and after a while the family was … say the truth of it, scared to be around him. Wasn't nobody shed no tears when they heard he'd been locked away. Abby was the youngest and she didn't hardly have no memories of Claude, he'd been gone so long.

"Yo, Claude," Shep said. Didn't get up or nothing. Wasn't no place to ask him to have a seat and Shep wouldn't have been inclined to offer him one if there had been. Shep was … what? Strange that now was the first time he'd noticed it. Shep was *on the sidelines*. Didn't seem to be up to him no more what he said or didn't say, nor what he done. Abby was the one deciding things now. The Abby that was in his head who didn't have Abby's bird-chirp voice.

Claude didn't seem to take offense at Shep's lack of a welcome. He just ducked his head and stepped through the hole in the wall, walked over to Shep and sat down in the dirt next to him.

He wasn't a big man, but he had always seemed big to Shep because there was an air of menace always hanging over him that made him appear bigger than he was. It was like he was one of them hand grenades you seen in the movies and he'd already removed that pin thing, grabbed that little circle with a piece of metal on the end with his teeth and yanked it out and was just holding onto the handle. And wouldn't take nothing at all, just the slightest provocation and Claude'd let go that handle and explode all over you and everybody else in the room.

He was covered in tattoos, most of them prison tats by somebody who couldn't draw. Wasn't a bare piece of skin anywhere Shep could see, except on his face, but there was skulls and daggers and such all tangled up together like a vine going up his neck to his chin.

His teeth was black stumps. But his eyes … Shep looked into his eyes and they was Abby's eyes, same color blue as hers, same dark eyelashes that made them stand out on his face.

"Won't nobody tell me what's goin' on." Claude spit out a splatter of tobacco juice. "But it's clear ain't nothing right."

"How'd you get out? I thought you's locked away for good." Shep was a little surprised his own self that he'd said something that forward and blunt.

Claude didn't seem to take offense, in fact it seemed like he warmed up to Shep because of it.

"Ain't rightly sure. My neighbors as was gonna testify made themselves a meth lab that blew up, killed half a dozen of them and then they wasn't no witnesses no more. Something like that. So they let me out and I come home … where is everybody?"

"Gone."

"Gone where?"

"Don't nobody know for sure."

"Why'd they leave?"

"Don't nobody know that neither."

Claude sat back and looked Shep up and down.

"Then what *do* you know?"

Abby started talking to Claude then outta Shep's mouth, told him all kinda things Shep didn't know about what had happened and why. And who was responsible. And what they'd ought to do about it. Claude and Shep both soaked up every word.

Chapter Fifteen

VIOLA WALKED SLOWLY from one room to the next in the Nower house — *her* house, now. Just looking, soaking it all up. She'd parked Essie in the rocking chair on the front porch and give her the old Barbie doll missing a leg that she hauled around with her everywhere. She'd be content to play with it for hours.

She was glad Neb, Obie and Zach hadn't got back yet. She didn't want them underfoot. They couldn't appreciate it, didn't know how to want things fine as these. They was just glad of indoor plumbing.

Malachi was the only one who'd know what a wonder it was, but she hadn't seen the boy in a couple a days and soon's she located him, she and him was going to have to have a Come-to-Jesus meeting. If it was true he'd cast his lot with Sam Sheridan and that prissy showoff — what was her name, Sylvia Ryan's youngest. Charlene. Viola very much did *not* like that young woman, they was challenge in them eyes and wasn't likely she was going to take to all that Viola had in mind. They was gonna butt heads, Viola was sure of it and hadn't never been a single time in her near seventy years on this earth that Viola Tackett butted heads with somebody and didn't leave them with they heads busted open. This one wouldn't be no different, but Viola had to have herself a talk with her youngest son, first.

Not now, though. She didn't want to do a single thing but wander around the castle that was now hers. On the first floor, then up to the second and then the third. Around and around she went.

The house was broke out with windows, big tall ones. Ceilings was probably sixteen feet and the windows was twelve — tall and thin, with sheer white curtains between the heavy velvet drapes, and the tops of all the windows was rounded, like the doorways that was archways from one big room into the next.

She remembered them sheers from when she was a little girl and tried to get a peek into the house, how she couldn't see anything but blurred shapes 'cause she was looking through that gauzy stuff. She went to one of the four bay windows on the front of the house, pulled the sheers back to let in the sun, meant to open them all up … but then she didn't. She let the sheers fall back into place. She wasn't on the outside looking in no more. She was on the inside looking out and now she was the one didn't want a bunch of nosey, prying eyes looking in on what she was doing.

She stood for so long staring at the crystal chandelier that hung over the cherry table in the dining room that she totally lost track of time. The room had red walls. They was an archway between the foyer and the dining room, and it had decorative spindles lined up at the top of it that was the same as the spindles in the staircase and the ones on the front porch railing. She reached out her hand and run it over the cherry tabletop.

In the parlor was an organ. A for-real organ.

When she walked out onto the landing to look down into the foyer from the third floor, she got all dizzy-like, had to grab the railing. She wasn't afraid of heights or nothing like that, but truth was she never did much like to stand on a high ridge, like Scott's Ridge or the cliff face on Bald Knob in Drayton County, looking out over the hollows. Made her stomach churn.

But that was fine, her stomach was doing backflips anyway as she wandered around her castle. When she's a little girl, she'd wanted to be a princess in this castle. But she'd had to wait her whole life, spent all the good years of it living hand to mouth, not nothing to show for all her effort. Wasn't until she was old that she finally come into her own and there was equal parts gratitude and resentment for that. Well, it'd took her a whole lifetime to get here and she sure as Jackson was gonna squeeze ever drop of juice outta the experience.

She wasn't no princess now, though. She was the queen and she decided right then and there that she wasn't going back home, back to the ugly little house where she'd been born on Gizzard Ridge out by Killarney. Decided she wasn't never gonna set foot in that place again. She'd send the boys to get her things, wasn't but a handful of things she wanted from there, anyway.

One day, she'd burn it down. She would light a match and pitch it in the door and stand outside and watch it go up in smoke. Sorry only that her daddy hadn't lived long enough to see it burn. Sorry that she couldn't have set him inside, maybe poured a little gasoline on him so's he'd catch quick.

She could have. Him like he was there at the end, she could have done anything she wanted to him. And she did.

The day they come to get her, saying something was

wrong with her daddy, she'd prayed the whole way to the hospital, begging God not to let him die. And on that fine day God'd done what the good book says, had given her more than she ever dared to ask or imagine.

Her father'd had a stroke, the doctors said. His whole right side was *paralyzed*, his face hung down, drooped, and his arm and leg just flopped. He couldn't hardly move his left side, neither, weak as a kitten he was. Best of all, though — he knew what was going on around him but *he couldn't talk*. He could see and understand, could feel it when you squeezed his hand. And when you stuck a needle down into his ear and watched the blood flow out.

She'd told them doctors her daddy wasn't gonna stay in no hospital, not when he had a family to take care of him. And she had brought the old man home to Nower County so's she and her sisters could see to him. They took turns, passed him from one to the other.

The terrified, haunted look in his eyes when she went to pick him up from one of her sisters' houses told her what she wanted to know, that they'd taken the opportunity to "see to daddy" just like she did, but she hadn't never asked.

His friends would come to visit him sometimes, sit and talk to him while she stood by, smiling. She'd watch him try to communicate, try to talk to them — desperate to communicate, his eyes begging for help. But wouldn't nothing come out his mouth but sounds that didn't make no sense, and she didn't never hurt him where nobody could see, of course. Was careful like that.

He lived less than a year and she made every second of it count. When he passed, she was the one to dress him before they put him in the coffin so wouldn't nobody see all the burns — some scarred over, some fresh. And after she got him dressed all nice and proper, didn't nobody notice that he didn't have no fingernails nor toenails, even though folks passed by real slow to say goodbye at the viewing. Didn't nobody but her sisters see he didn't have no privates no more, neither, and nary a one of them ever mentioned it to her. Viola'd been the one got rid of his "manhood." Real slow. Piece by piece.

But she surely did wish he'd lived long enough for her to burn him up in his own house, lying in the bed where he'd done what he'd done to her — it was her earliest clear memory so she musta been two or three years old. Kept at it, done her and her sisters night after night, year after year. Wasn't nothing terrible enough to do to him to pay for that. But she hadn't never in her life considered longer or harder on what she *could* do, and she made sure everything she done counted.

Burning him alive in that bed woulda been the icing on the cake, but he had denied his daughters that final gift, and that was a pure shame, for a fact.

Suddenly, the front door flew open and all three of her sons lumbered in like cows coming home to the barn.

"We got him, Mama," Neb bawled. "Locked him up in the jail just like you said."

"You done tracked mud all over the floor," she cried, and the boys looked down like they'd just now noticed for the first time in their lives that they had feet. "Get on out of here!" She shooed them right back out the way they'd come in. "And don't you come back 'til you've cleaned up yore boots!"

Soon's they was something resembling presentable, she made them sandwiches from the big jar of peanut butter she found in the pantry where Mr. Nower had hoarded up all kinda food, enough to feed her and hers for a month of Sundays. Not that it mattered. Wouldn't have made no never mind if the pantry hadn't had nothing in it but a sack of flour full of weevils. She'd take whatever she wanted whenever she wanted it from whoever had it. She wasn't never again gonna have to worry about having enough to eat.

Then she sent Neb and Obie to the courthouse to set her up in the sheriff's office, and see if they couldn't talk Betty Greenleaf, the dispatcher, into *volunteering* to stay on under the new … administration.

Then she got Zach to put out a message over the phone tree — didn't have to go nowhere because there was a phone right there in the Nower House — the *Tackett* House! Two phones, in fact, one upstairs and one downstairs. She made him repeat what he was supposed to say three times, so's he wouldn't screw it up.

Since Viola hadn't never had a telephone, she didn't have nobody to call and she dearly would like to do that. Just pick up the phone and talk to somebody, easy as you please. Didn't want the boys around watching when she done it, though, in case she didn't get it right the first try. She'd wait until Neb got to the courthouse and then call the sheriff's office, make up some reason so he wouldn't know she was just playing with the phone like a little kid with a new Christmas toy.

She smiled broadly, revealing the space between her two front teeth.

Chapter Sixteen

TOBY WITHERSPOON FOUND the proof he needed as soon as he stopped looking for it.

The only thing the boy knew about proof and crimes and such came from the cop shows he watched on television back when television sets still worked. Back before J-Day. He lived on the outskirts of the Ridge, so he got pretty good reception, the ridge being in a good-sized hollow where the surrounding mountains didn't block the signal, at least not all the time.

His favorite cop show was *NYPD Blue* and he watched it religiously, never missed an episode. His favorite character, as unlikely as it seemed, was Andy Sipowicz. The reason Toby liked him so much was because he wasn't perfect. He wasn't the usual hero who was handsome and always got his man and all the girls wanted to take him home to their apartments "for a drink, later …"

He actually reminded Toby of his father, and he had trouble reconciling the reality that he hated his father with how much he loved the television character who drank on the job, and was a negative bigot — didn't like women, except for the drink-later part, which none of them ever invited him to, or black people or gay people or … he was mostly negative about everything.

Which was just like Toby's father.

Except Sipowicz managed to make all those characteristics okay. Toby admired him because he kept going even when life wasn't good, even when he didn't get the girl or got caught drinking or … well, there was the time he got shot by somebody he'd made fun of earlier.

Mostly Toby admired him because he was so good at his job. He was what the other characters called "a cop's cop," which Toby took to mean the best of the best. He had watched Sipowicz solve crimes, watched how he found evidence, followed the clues and caught the bad guys.

So when Toby set out to prove that his father had killed his mother, it wasn't like he didn't know how to do that. He did, knew his was an uphill battle because he lacked the key things all the cop shows used to catch the bad guys.

He didn't have a … body.

The first time he'd thought of it that way, of his mother as a body, he went into the bathroom and threw up, coughed and gagged, stuff coming out of his nose and acid burning up the back off his throat.

But after he got that out of his system, he was able to kinda pretend it was somebody else's body, not his mother. Didn't matter whose body it was, though, he didn't have one. Which meant there was no way to take a bullet out of the body and compare it to a gun and determine that was the murder weapon, because of those marks on the bullet, scratches made on it when it was fired down the gun barrel.

Without a body, there was no way to even prove she was dead, let alone murdered. And not just murdered, but murdered by his father.

So he tried to think about it like Sipowicz would. What would he do? If he thought somebody'd been murdered, there had to be a reason. Toby knew his mother had been murdered because she'd been home on J-Day. Toby had seen her, though he feared he might have been the only person who had and he didn't think that kind of evidence would go very far. But his father went around telling people that her sister had come to get her and the two of them were shopping for shoes in Lexington and his mother got caught outside the Jabberwock mirage.

What Sipowicz would do, Toby thought, was work with what he had instead of moping around about what he didn't have. His mother had been home on J-Day. Was there any way to prove that? She had not gone shoe shopping with her sister like his father said. Was there any way to prove that? Was there any evidence that his father had lied about the whereabouts of his mother?

Toby had spent days thinking about it and was no closer to figuring it out than when he started.

And what did the condition of his father when he came home last night have to do with his mother's murder? Maybe it didn't have anything to do with it. Maybe it was some other thing altogether — something bad, though, because his father was trying to cover it up. He had taken the clothes he'd been wearing, the ones that were covered in blood, out to the trash barrel last night where they'd be burned up. Why didn't he just wash out the blood? It was odd — suspicious — so Toby'd retrieved the garments from the garbage first thing this morning and stuck them in the back of the woodpile. Then he had set the trash on fire. His father'd been mad about that. Toby wasn't ever supposed to burn the trash. His mother'd been afraid he would catch his clothing on fire. His father didn't have nearly as many rules about Toby's behavior as his mother'd had, and actually had already been so drunk by the time he realized the trash was on fire that he had done little but yell at Toby and call him stupid.

His father was probably using the alcohol to dull the pain, which Toby suspected was pretty bad. Black eye, swollen nose that was probably broken, busted lip, and his front tooth was chipped, had a big hunk knocked out of it. He'd told Toby he fell down some stairs, then went off into his den to read sports magazines and get drunker.

Toby was just about to make himself a sandwich for lunch when he took Custard out to do her business and she got off the leash. Custard had been his mother's dog, a yappy little beast from the animal shelter that didn't do much of anything except bark and dig holes in the backyard and sit in his mother's lap while she was reading.

The dog would have starved to death after J-Day if it hadn't been for Toby. No, she wouldn't have lived long enough to starve because his father would have killed her for making messes on the floor when nobody took her out.

Toby didn't like the dog, but he didn't want it to die, either, so he'd taken over responsibility for the animal. He hadn't been careful that evening when he took her out, didn't fasten the leash properly on her collar and as soon as she had squatted, done her do and kicked dirt over it with her hind feet, she'd run off.

There was no catching Custard if she didn't want to be caught, so Toby didn't bother to try. She'd come home when she got hungry. Or she wouldn't. He was okay with it either way. And sure enough, she'd come scratching at the back door while Toby was eating his sandwich. When he opened the door, he found the dog on the back porch with something she'd dug up in the yard. It was covered in dirt, but Toby instantly recognized it.

It was his *mother's purse.*

He let the dog in, took the purse and hurried upstairs to the bathroom to clean it up. It was leather, so the dirt came off easy, and it'd been zipped up so the contents were untouched. His mother's wallet was inside, with her credit cards and the extra set of car keys to the Ford. Her asthma inhaler was there as well.

His mother would not have driven off with her sister to go buy shoes — without her purse and wallet. And she never went anywhere without her inhaler.

Toby sat on the side of the tub, looking at the purse he'd cleaned off and set on the closed toilet lid beside him.

This was *proof*, wasn't it? Proof even Sipowicz would have bought. But it was only proof that his mother hadn't gone to Lexington. It wasn't proof that his father had killed her. How could Toby …?

Toby froze. Custard had come into the bathroom behind him and he'd locked her in with him, and now he sat staring at the dog, wondering.

There was a big compost pile behind the garage. It'd been his mother's idea, said it would keep the septic tank from getting stopped up and they could use it for fertilizer on her flowers. Toby had helped her dig the hole. It was only about three feet deep.

She was the only one who took stuff out and dumped it there. He hadn't been there since she left. What if …?

Maybe that's where Custard had dug up her purse. And maybe that's where … He couldn't do it. Absolutely, one hundred percent could not do it. He could not go out there with a shovel and try to dig up …

Toby shivered. He didn't have to, though, did he? Didn't he have enough evidence for "probably cause," to get somebody to search the property, somebody to dig up the compost heap behind the garage?

Right, and who might that be?

The sheriff, of course. They lived close enough to town that Toby could ride his bike there. He could take his mother's purse to the sheriff's office, show it to him, tell him how his daddy beat up his mother all the time and how she had been home — *he had seen her!* — on J-Day.

Toby got up and wrapped the purse in a big bath towel, left the bathroom and shoved the towel and purse under his bed. He would wait until his father was very drunk, asleep on the couch, and then he would get on his bike and take his mother's purse to the sheriff, convince him to come find the "evidence" he feared was buried in a grave behind the garage.

Chapter Seventeen

As soon as Pete seen Charlie with Merrie beside her mama's car, he rushed — for Pete, it was "rushing" — across the parking lot to be a gentleman and help her find whatever it was she was looking for. She was down on her knees beside the open back door, digging around under the front passenger seat and came up with a red crayon just as he got there to help.

Though he'd changed his mind about it a dozen times on the walk from his house to the clinic, he understood he had to tell her what he'd seen on the map in his living room, that crazy as it was, she had a right to know.

"'Lo, Pete," she said when he approached.

"Dog!" Merrie squealed, ran to the animal and threw her arms around his neck. He bore her effusiveness with dignity. "Mr. Rufford, can we play wiff the water hose? Squirt it up to the sky?"

"Might be we'll do just that," he told her, "but I need to talk to your mama a bit first."

Charlie had obviously picked up on the look on his face — the look of a man who had something weighing on him. Or maybe just the look of a man who hadn't had no appetite to speak of in over a week, so's he'd already had to cinch up his belt two loops.

Or the look of a man who was … dying.

Dang, he hated that word. Sounded so whiney. But it was what it was.

Charlie handed Merrie the crayon.

"Take this inside and finish coloring your picture. I'll be right behind you."

"It's a red duck," she told Pete. "Not a yellow one. Yellow ducks are boring."

Then she turned and headed into the building. Charlie closed the car door and leaned against it.

"'S'up?"

Wasn't no easy way to say it so he just put it out there, plain.

"Your husband's name wouldn't happen to be Stuart, would it?" The look of shock on her face was all the answer he needed. "'Cause if it is, I think maybe me and him had ourselves a little chat this morning."

He told her the story, the condensed version anyway, then she hauled him into the building, said she wanted him to tell the whole thing all over again to Sam Sheridan — and Malachi Tackett, who looked rode hard and put up wet, like maybe he'd had a bad night. Pete hadn't been at last night's county meeting but had heard all about it, about pool Liam! Maybe Malachi's appearance had something to do with his mama taking over the whole county.

"Welcome to the Breakfast Club," Malachi said as he sipped what looked like a cup full of road tar. "But the only role left to play is that idiot teacher and you don't fit the part at all."

"I ain't got no idea what you just said."

"Never mind, it's a movie—"

"Don't do movies. Television, neither."

"Sit down, Pete," Sam said. "You don't look good."

Pete wanted to fire back that she didn't look so hot herself, but it wasn't true. Sam Sheridan was a beautiful woman — wholesome beautiful, and he hadn't never seen her that she didn't look scrubbed-up-clean gorgeous.

Charlie tossed the words out into the room like a hand grenade.

"Pete talked to Stuart this morning, too." *Too?* "Tell them, Pete."

So Pete told them. The room was silent when he finished and he wanted to ask what Charlie'd meant, but let it go for later.

Malachi was the first to recover. Recognition flowed over his face and he asked Charlie, "*Stuart McClintock*? I just put it together. Is your husband *the*—?"

"Pittsburgh Steelers — yes," she said.

Pete didn't know what a football team had to do with anything, but he let that go for later, too.

"You tried to do it again, you say?" Malachi asked. "Tried to send another 'message'?"

"Yup, stuck pins all over that map, then stood there waiting, but didn't no other ones appear. Way I got it figured … and of course this is so crazy it don't mean nothing—"

"You're going to have to take the oath, too," Sam said.

Sam made an X motion across her heart with her right hand and then held it up in an I-swear position. "We've made an agreement that we don't censor what we tell each other because we think whatever it is we've experienced is too nutty to be believable. These days in Nower County, everything's believable."

That was a smart thing to do and Pete felt some of the tension drain away.

"Deal." He made the same X motion across his heart. "So what I figured was there was ... *something* there in the beginning when I first got home. Dog was all bent outta shape over it, went postal — if you'll forgive an old mail carrier a little post office humor. And soon's whatever it was left ... I don't know, the door shut, maybe."

"Door shut?" Charlie asked. You could tell she was real tore up over what Pete'd told her but was struggling to hold herself together.

"The doorway ... the link ... passageway ..." Pete offered. "I'd say 'portal,' but then we'd all start hearing the theme song from *The Twilight Zone*."

"Okay, door," Charlie said. "But the door to *where?*"

"I don't think we can figure out where the door leads *to* until we have some understanding of where it leads *from*," Malachi said. "Here. Where we are? Where exactly is *that?*"

"It shore as Jackson ain't Nower County, Kentucky," Pete found himself saying, and felt the truth of the words as they left his lips.

No one said anything, like maybe they'd been thinking the same thing, but it was a lot more powerful a thought when you heard it coming out of somebody else's mouth.

"Not the real one, anyway. It's ... made up, but whoever, *whatever* made it up didn't get all the details right."

"But how can that be?" Sam almost wailed the words.

"Let's skip the how part for now," Malachi suggested, "and concentrate on the what. I think we are in Nower County." He turned to Pete. "I think you were in your living room this morning in Nower County, Kentucky. And I think ... there was *somebody else* in your house this morning, too. At the same time you were there. That somebody else was Stuart McClintock."

"Whoa, Bessie, let's pull this wagon back up to the

barn and start loading it all over again," Pete said. "Slow. You sayin' you think I was in my living room and Stuart McClintock was also in my living room at the same time, but we couldn't see each other?"

"You got any other explanation for how those stickpins just appeared?"

"But how could—?" Sam began.

"We're skipping the how for now, remember," Malachi said. "All the questions that begin with how have the same answer: the Jabberwock."

"So … I was in my living room, and Charlie's husband, Stuart, was also in my living room at the same time" — Charlie looked like she was ready to cry — "but we couldn't … connect with each other?"

"That would mean Stuart was also in my kitchen yesterday," Charlie said. "Is that what you think — that Stuart was—?"

"Had to be," Malachi said, then turned to Pete. "Actually, you *could* connect with each other — at least briefly. As long as the door was open—"

"As long as Dog was barking at—"

"At the Jabberwock," Malachi said. "The Jabberwock was there, the Jabberwock that's in our world. It was obviously in … the other world, the other Nower County in your living room … at the same time. And in Charlie's kitchen yesterday. The Jabberwock is the door."

"When it left, the door closed."

"So the only way to connect to … to the real world out there is through the Jabberwock?" Sam asked.

"Sounds like it," Malachi said.

"Goody." It was all Pete could say, didn't have no air to say anything else.

Silence flowed into the room, heavy and oppressive.

Then Malachi got to his feet. "I suggest we go have us a little chat with the Jabberwock."

"Go sit at the county line and talk to our reflections?" Sam asked.

"No." He turned to Charlie. "I say we go to Charlie's house and write the chap a letter." Pete's face musta looked as confused as he felt so Malachi told him about the words that'd appeared on Charlie's blackboard this morning. "We need to figure out what game we're playing and the J-dude is the only one who knows. Maybe he'll show up and we can be pen pals."

Chapter Eighteen

THE WORLD WHIRLED AROUND CHARLIE. Malachi was suggesting they all go to her house and see if they could get the Jabberwock to chat with them through the blackboard in her kitchen.

Charlie was struggling to stay in the here-and-now while inside her mind a klaxon cry was echoing off the insides of her skull.

Stuart was here!

Okay, not *here* here. But here nonetheless.

Stuart had come looking for her.

He really had!

Charlie didn't have anywhere inside to put a revelation like that. It was such an enormous concept that when she tried to stuff it into her head she could feel pieces of it dangling out her ears.

She'd told herself that the "message" she'd gotten from Stuart yesterday morning was just her own yearning, that she'd written the words herself. She pretty much had herself convinced that was true until the chalked message appeared on her blackboard *from the Jabberwock.*

She probably hadn't slept more than half an hour last night trying to process the implications of the two messages, still denying in her heart of hearts that Stuart really had written the first one.

Now, there was no denying it. He had written the first message on her kitchen blackboard yesterday and a second in stick-pins on Pete's map this morning.

She had kept it together rather well, she thought, was right proud of herself that she didn't collapse in a puddle when Pete told her about it in the veterinary hospital parking lot.

Your husband's name wouldn't happen to be Stuart, would it?

And the word "Stuart" had gone off like a fifty-megaton nuclear warhead in her mind.

She had tried to contribute in a meaningful way to all the conversation that followed, because it was important — a "breakthrough" for the Breakfast Club, whose members had banded together to try to solve the Jabberwock mystery before E.J. died of rabies ... and before the monster absorbed everybody in the county. Getting some kind of communication from "the outside world," even if it was in as bizarre a fashion as stickpins on a map, was huge.

But that "huge" was a mouse among elephants compared to the revelation that Stuart *really had* come looking for Charlie.

No doubt about it this time.

He'd written his name in stickpins on Pete's map, for crying out loud. It was real.

And her response to that revelation somehow managed to be equal parts ecstasy and devastation. She didn't want to care! She had put him out of her mind, had "divorced" herself from him emotionally in the days following the shattering discovery of the credit card statement and the phone call to Hawaii. She would have returned to

Clarendon Hills after cleaning out her mother's house to begin the legal side of that process. She hadn't let herself consider that part, though, not yet.

Perhaps it was because Charlie was a writer, was used to compartmentalizing the lives of several people in her head at the same time. Maybe that's what made her able to take what had happened when she spoke to the desk clerk at the Oahu Marriott — "Mr. and Mrs. McClintock have already left" — and seal it away in its own little box. She fully intended to open up that box as soon as she got back home and when she did, she would have to confront Stuart. They would have to ... what? *Discuss it.* Seriously? No, thank you very much, she had no intention of discussing anything. What they would have to do was start the arduous task of ripping apart their marriage.

File divorce papers.

Given that the person she'd be suing for divorce was an attorney, it could get ugly. And what about Merrie?

But when she'd come home to Kentucky to sort out her mother's belongings and straighten up the details of her life, she had stuffed all those considerations into the box and had given herself permission not to think about any of what lay ahead. One step at a time. Settle her mother's affairs. Arrange for the sale of what it had taken her mother a lifetime to accumulate, belongings that didn't mean anything to anybody but Sylvia Ryan. Charlie had even set up a time out there in the future when she would allow herself to consider what was about to happen next.

Not until she'd boarded the plane in Lexington bound for O'Hare Airport in Chicago, had settled into her seat, had occupied Merrie with a coloring book, had accepted the obligatory soft drink and package of three peanuts — *only then* would she open up the box. *Not until.*

She had made an emotional survival strategy much like that of Scarlett O'Hara. "I'll think about that tomorrow."

But then Jabberwock gobbled up all the tomorrows. The shiny mirage cinched tight around the county had stopped time. The Jabberwock had screwed all that to a tree.

And in so doing, it had granted her a reprieve. During the strange time here in limbo, she had left the box where it sat, locked safely away in the back of her mind, a bomb that would destroy her whole world when she opened it. But just sitting there. Ticking.

Then the old man with the shaggy beard had peered at her with kind eyes this morning.

Your husband's name wouldn't happen to be Stuart, would it?

And the contents of that box *rumbled*. Wile E. Coyote lights the fuse on a little black ball, drops it into a box and closes the lid and the explosion makes the box dance in place.

The husband who had been playing bump and tickle with another woman on a beach in Hawaii ... had come looking for Charlie.

Stuart had come to Kentucky to find her.

Why?

What did he want?

To tell her he wanted a divorce so he and Whatever-hernamewas could live happily ever after? He could have done that on the phone. In fact, a message like that was much safer delivered from a distance.

Then what *did* he want?

She was spared the task of puzzling that out. Before the Breakfast Club members even left the breakroom, Raylynn poked her head in and announced, "I just got a call from my aunt. She said Viola Tackett's at the court-house about to start a trial."

"Trial?" Malachi asked.

"She's charged Dylan Shaw with murdering his grand-mother, Martha Whittiker. And Viola's going to be the judge ... and the jury, too, I guess."

Chapter Nineteen

VIOLA TRIED to look like she was listening to that Shaw kid's meandering tale of woe, how he hadn't done nothing, didn't kill his pore ol' granny and didn't know who did — with side rants about how he'd been treated by her boys, how Obie'd punched him in the face and blacked his eye and Neb'd kicked him when he fell down so hard in the back that he was peeing blood. Sniveling the whole time, snot running down his nose either because he was bawling or because he was coming down off crack and that'd make anybody's nose run something fierce.

And maybe he hadn't killed her. Who knew? They was folks thought he did it and that was all that was important. And Viola'd planted folks at last night's meeting to make it look like half the county was scared whoever killed Martha Whittiker was gonna sneak into their houses in the middle of the night and bash their heads in like he done hers.

Didn't matter who really had killed that poor old lady. Viola had caught Dylan Shaw and if he wasn't the doer, well he'd just have to take one for the team, sacrifice himself for the greater good of Viola Tackett and her boys.

He stood before her in the big county courtroom, where a big crowd was slowly beginning to gather, courtesy of Zach's announcement on the phone tree. Not having no telephone herself, Viola only had a vague idea how that thing worked. Somebody called and give you a message, and you called other folks — something like that. The county meeting had been testimony to the fact the thing didn't work perfect because wasn't no way the whole county showed up. But this little event might be better attended. It was something folks would *want* to see.

Hadn't nobody shown up yet who was like to cause any trouble, though after Liam Montgomery got hisself shot at the meeting last night and she'd had no choice but to step forward and restore order, she suspected weren't many left who'd give Viola Tackett any grief. Oh, there was folks who probably wasn't going to like what was about to happen. Dylan Shaw's mother had run off years ago and he didn't have no people left here except the grandmother he either offed or didn't.

But they was others, folks of "high morals," like that preacher Reverend Norman, whose face always looked so pinched he musta spent his life walking around with a wedgie. He'd been one of the first to show up at the court-house, but he didn't appear to be as interested in the goings on as he was in questioning everybody who came in. Seems he'd misplaced his daughter, the fat one who'd shown up in the Middle of Nowhere blind on J-Day. She hadn't come home last night and sounded like he'd spent the whole night trying to find her.

And Big Ed, a man who stood six-ten if he was a foot, a rival doper who didn't give a rip about the Shaw kid but who would be liable to start trouble just because he was smart enough to figure out that once Viola was in charge, his little dope operation was toast.

Mrs. Throckmorton, the crazy cat lady from the far side of Bishop Mountain who'd made it her life's mission to provide a home for every litter of stray cats in every barn in the county was so softhearted she wouldn't have approved of giving the kid a spanking. And they was others like her out there, just simple folks who "didn't want no trouble," wouldn't want to see the violence they was about to witness but too gutless to try to put a stop to it.

Viola sat up on that raised platform in the big judge's chair, that she'd had to roll up all the way to the top to be tall enough so's she could see out over that desk thing where they was supposed to be a gavel that she could bang to make people shut up and listen. Gavel was gone. So was the benches where the spectators was supposed to sit out behind that railing that separated them from the "officers of the county." The prosecutor, county attorney, and the defense attorneys, sitting on opposite sides of the room. Least that's the way it was the times she'd been in this courtroom, and that was more times than she liked to remember, there to get her boys or her crew out of one mess or another.

Courthouse had been closed for years, but there had still been a functioning sheriff's department, though how that was she couldn't imagine, 'less it was something paid for from all that grant money foundations and such was always throwing at the "poor folks" in the mountains. With the sheriff's department in the basement, the rest of the courthouse was mostly let be. It was all empty, 'course, all the offices, furniture was gone, drapes and curtains and shades took off the windows. But hadn't been hardly any vandalism a'tall. And the things that couldn't be picked up and moved — like the judge's desk and that railing thing — they was still there. The benches, the prosecutor's table and where the defense sat, the chairs for the jury — all that was gone. So was the little desk and chair where that court reporter sat — her name was Selma Spinnett and she'd clicked away at that little machine every day for forty years.

She hadn't never typed in the name of Viola Tackett, though. Not once. Viola's record was squeaky clean as a newborn chick! She hadn't never been caught doing nothing! Not in a whole lifetime spent on the wrong side of the law. Oh, she woulda been hauled into this courtroom in cuffs and then off to do time in the Kentucky Correctional Institution for Women in Peewee Valley a dozen times over the years if one of hers had ever been willing to rat her out. And don't think them prosecutors didn't try to talk them into it — here and in Marion County, Nelson County, Harlan County and neighboring Beaufort, Crawford and Drayton counties. Once, her crew'd got caught and ended up in federal court in Lexington. But didn't nobody ever point the finger at Viola. Not one of them, not a single time. They wasn't a big bunch of folks — didn't take a whole lot of people to work the business she run. They was a small crew but a mighty one and loyal to the bone.

It put her in mind of what that circuit-riding preacher'd said in a sermon once when she was a kid, talking about Jesus's disciples. He'd said the proof that they hadn't made up their story about all the miracles He done was that they stuck to it to the end, ever last one of them, even when they was tortured and crucified and fed to lions and such. And she b'lieved that, b'lieved they hadn't made the whole thing up, but the fact that they stuck to their stories wasn't proof of that. That's what loyal people done, they stuck to those they's loyal to. Hers done the same for her, and because they did, they knew she'd look after their families while they's away. She'd see to it there was food on the table and coats and shoes for the kids in the wintertime.

She didn't never let none of those that was loyal to her down, not in almost half a century of being in charge. And they knew it'd be the same now that she was in charge — really in charge, running the whole kit and caboodle all by her lonesome. They knew she'd look after them same's she always done. So when she'd reached out to 'em, said she was looking for Dylan Shaw, they rolled over and coughed him up quick.

Now he was standing there looking up at her — that's what that raised platform was for, so's them as was accused of wrongdoing had to look up at the folks sitting in judgment. She'd long ago figured out that it was planned that way, psychological persuasion. It was all set up to let them on the wrong side of the law know they was outgunned from the git-go.

Which put her in mind of that movie, *Cool Hand Luke*, the one with Paul Newman where he was on a prison farm but wouldn't bow to authority or to the system … and consequently got the crap beat out of him over and over. Viola never seen that movie the way other folks did. They was all over the Paul Newman character, oohing and aahing over how … *cool* he was, admired his courage and what they called his "indominable" spirit. Viola thought that whole thing was a pile of the warm sticky stuff you found on the south side of a jackass heading north. Yeah he was brave, but he was way more stupid than brave. How dumb do you have to be to set yourself up on one side with a whole prison full of guards and a mean-as-a-snake warden on the other? All he got for his trouble was pain, prancing around all defiant-like, feeling superior to all the rest of the folks because he'd decided he just flat out was not going to play in their reindeer games.

In the end, they killed him for it. What was the point in that? And them inmates talking about him after he was dead, exaggerating whatever he done until they made him into some kinda superhero. That was all well and good for that Dragline character who was so impressed by him. But Luke? Luke was a corpse moldering in a grave, worms a eating at his insides.

And he *picked* it. Stuck his chest out like some kinda banty rooster and dared the rest of them to knock that stupid lopsided smile off'n his face.

Idiot!

Now if it'd been Viola, she'd a played the game a whole lot smarter. She'd a'seen what side her bread was buttered on quick. She'd a sucked up to that captain fella, woulda traded information for special privileges — decent food and a good bed, woulda rode out her sentence in the best circumstances possible. And she'd a walked outta there a free woman when she'd served her time — with time off for good behavior, of course. She'd a been out there smelling the roses and chasing butterflies or getting drunk or finding her a good man to shack up with for about a week to make up for all the time she'd gone without. She sure as Jackson wouldn't a been dead.

If they was anybody to be admired in that movie, it was the captain. He was just as determined as Luke, had the same kinda iron will. 'Cept he started out on the winning side and he knew it. And he won. In the end it was him told them folks to drive Luke to the hospital "real slow," so's he'd have time to bleed to death on the way.

It was him she was thinking about while the kid in front of her whined and sniveled and alternated between begging for mercy and claiming that he was innocent. Whiny, lowlife coward that he was, he was still like Cool Hand Luke in one respect. He didn't get it. He was operating under the misapprehension that he had some say about what happened to him, that he could convince Viola

Tackett he didn't do it and then she'd say, "Oh, you's innocent? Well, pardon me. I'm sorry I inconvenienced you like I done, sending my boys to dig you out from under that chicken house where you's hiding."

He didn't understand that his fate was sealed soon's Viola settled on him to use as an example of her authority and absolute power. Soon's she picked him, he was good as dead.

When he shut up his whining to get a breath, she so wanted to say to him what that Captain had said to Luke, the line out of the movie everybody quoted. "What we got here is a failure to communicate."

She didn't say it, though. He wouldn't a got it. She'd just let him babble on for awhile 'til there was a decent crowd of people in the courtroom. Soon's there was, she'd come down on him with both feet.

Chapter Twenty

E.J. Stephenson had never dreamed the human body could endure the kind of agony he felt and survive. Surely the pain itself, regardless of the wound that had caused it, would be sufficient to cause death. E.J. could feel his screams making his throat raw and the sound was a vibration in his ears. But for some reason he couldn't actually hear the sounds, just felt them.

In his crazy reality of waking dreams, he was both the man on the bed in agony, and an objective observer. Dr. Elijah Stephenson, Doctor of Veterinary Medicine, LLC. The good doctor could no longer remember what the letters LLC stood for, but he could make accurate observations about the raving lunatic who was writhing in agony on the bed.

The man was hot. Why? Did he have a fever? A fever was not a symptom of rabies and even if it were, he wouldn't be developing symptoms yet. It would be several days yet — he was no longer sure how many — before the rabies virus began eating him alive from the inside, digesting the nuclei of his brain cells and reducing him to an unresponsive puddle of goo.

Or making him violent. So he'd have to be chained up to keep him from hurting somebody.

Oh dear holy God, what if he bit somebody and gave them rabies?

The thought so totally horrified him that both the E.J. Stephensons were shocked into silence — the lunatic in agony and the clinical observer who'd been watching him. Both of them froze in place, then settled as one into the pain-wracked body on the bed, gasping for air.

"Are you okay now? You were moaning and crying out, thrashing around."

Raylynn. It was Raylynn's voice, but he'd never heard it sound like that before.

Or had he? Had he heard her voice sound tender and caring and … loving — was that loving? — any number of times before but he had blown right by it. Why was it he was able to stop, absorb and appreciate it now when he'd never noticed?

Maybe it was the dying. Dying, as he understood, did strange things to a person.

He opened his eyes and Raylynn looked down at him, concern coupled with exhaustion stapled in a pleat between her eyebrows — that seemed to wing up at both ends, framing her startling gray eyes. Her eyes were arresting, set against her black skin. Stunning, really.

"E.J.?"

He hadn't answered her, found that he was having difficulty forming coherent words that conveyed meaning from one human being to another.

"I'm good." It was all he could say, but it was enough to reassure her so she let go of his arm. Had she been holding him on the bed? He didn't think he'd had another seizure like this morning, but maybe he needed restraints. He would eventually, would have to be tied down like … well, like a mad dog.

What if he bit Raylynn?

He convulsively clamped his teeth so tightly shut his jaw muscles instantly began to cramp and his teeth hurt.

"You need to … stay back," he croaked, and realized then that his dry throat and mouth were what was causing his difficulty speaking. "… drink? Could I have a …?"

She had the cup to his lips before he got the end of the sentence out and he tried to gulp down great swallows of liquid. But she wouldn't let him, only offered it for measured sips. As many as he wanted, but measured sips.

When his tongue no longer felt like it was affixed to the roof of his mouth like a piece of Velcro, he settled back and focused, tried to see Raylynn clearly.

He knew exactly where he was on the rollercoaster ride from hell. The one that started in agony totally unbearable, went through the valley of narcotic ease and then started back up the slope to the zenith not far ahead.

Sam had given him pills after the seizure. Those were wearing off now, but he was still lucid. He had to speak.

"You have to stay away, Raylynn. You … all of you."

She smiled and patted his arm, like he was a four-year-old who'd just said a word he didn't know the definition of.

"Listen to me." He grabbed her wrist and gripped with all the strength he had, which wasn't much but enough to show her he meant business. "I'm not contagious … yet. But when I am … there's no way to tell exactly when that will be — you have to protect yourselves. I might … bite you."

Her eyes welled with tears.

"You're not going to be biting anybody because you're

not going to get rabies because we're going to get you out of here and get you a vaccination and—"

"Hush." He said the word softly and she cut off in mid-reassurance.

"I could infect you … any of you. And I would rather die than—"

"Don't say that. You're not going to—"

"Yes I am." He squeezed the wrist he was still holding and tried to pull her toward him. He was too weak, but she went in the direction he pulled. "I *am* going to die."

"No, you—"

"Stop it. You're not helping. Please be real. Please …"

He hadn't meant for his voice to break, but it did, and it broke Raylynn with it. Her eyes welled with tears so quickly they squirted down her cheeks. And though she shook her head slowly back and forth in denial, the words she spoke were acceptance.

"Okay, you're going … to die." She took a breath. "There. I've said it. Now, will you lie back and try to relax and—"

"I don't want to die of rabies."

"Of course you don't, and we're trying—"

"Will you do that for me, Raylynn? Promise me that you won't let me die of rabies."

"E.J., I would do *anything* … but I can't get you out of—"

"You can keep me from dying of rabies, though. You can, Raylynn. You know you can."

He stared into her eyes, his eyes begging her to understand. It dawned on her slowly and horror raced denial to take over her face.

"E.J., no! Don't say … don't even *think*—"

"I am about to die like a mad dog, foaming at the

mouth, maybe chewing off my own limbs, locked in a cage so I can't hurt you … you want a front row seat for that?"

He hadn't meant to be harsh but … well, reality was harsh.

"No, E.J., but—"

"Then help me. Please, help me."

He pulled her as close as he could with the phantom of strength.

"I've never needed anything more in my life than I need this now. And you're my only hope. Please, Raylynn." His voice broke then and he began to cry, not sob, though. He didn't have the strength to sob. He just lay there, his chest hitching up and down, tears running down his temples and into his ears.

She was crying, too, but she wasn't making any noise. Silent tears streamed down her face, to drip off her chin.

He barely heard her speak. Her voice was a whisper on a breath.

"I'll help you, E.J. I'll help."

Chapter Twenty-One

IT TOOK JUST about the whole afternoon to put on a show of it. Viola'd sent the boys out to gather up the "witnesses," so's they could come stand before her and tell her what they'd seen. They hauled in Wilbur Berg, who'd been the one to find the body. He was either so scared or so excited to be there that he didn't make a whole lot of sense. If she'd really cared what he had to say, she'd a made him stop, slow down, begin at the front and tell the story straight through. But what he said didn't mean beans. He coulda said that he'd seen a spaceship land in the backyard and aliens got out of it and bashed in Martha Whittiker's head, and it wouldn't have made no never mind.

Viola just let him talk.

He said he'd told the whole thing to Liam when he come, and she put a sad look on her face then and said it was a shame Liam wasn't here to tell the court about it. Then she put a stern look on her face and told the growing crowd that she was gonna find whoever it was that shot Liam, she was gonna haul them in here into this court-room and they was gonna get what they deserved.

And she would do that if she had to. She didn't think she would. She was sure that with Liam getting shot, and her stepping in instantly and taking charge — and demonstrating that she meant business by dispensing "justice" on a kid who'd kill his own grandma … no, she wouldn't likely get any guff from anybody. But if they did need more convincing, she'd find somebody to blame Liam's murder on, haul them in here and dispense "justice" on them, too.

Oh, how she wished she could blame it on Sylvia Ryan's girl, that Charlie McClintock. Trouble was, the whole crowd knew she was in the back of the room holding her kid when the shot was fired, they all seen her run in there and kneel beside the body so they was no way to hang it on her.

That was okay, though. Viola'd see to Miss Pretty soon enough. That girl would rue the day she ever dared to cross Viola Tackett right there in public, defy her with people standing there watching. Oh, she would very much regret that she'd ever done such a thing. Viola already had a plan in mind, was still figuring out the particulars. Soon's she had it all mapped out, she would go after that woman and make that little girl of hers an orphan quick. Maybe she'd say the line to her, what that captain said in that movie. When she was standing there denying she done whatever it was Viola'd trumped up to charge her with, maybe even being defiant to the end. She struck Viola as the same kind of stupid as Luke was. Proud stupid. Defiant stupid. All cocky and unbreakable stupid.

Maybe she'd look Miss Fancy Pants in the face and say, even put on a southern accent and say the words like that captain done. "What we got here" — pronounced *he-ah* — "is a *fail-yore* to *comun-cate*."

That woman'd get the reference, know where it come from. And if she was as smart as she seemed to think she was, she might even figure out what Viola meant by using it. Might get the message: I'm in charge, you ain't. Cross me and this is what you get.

Viola smiled a little, imagining it, imagining saying them words, when she looked up and dang if that woman wasn't standing right there in the courtroom. Had just come in and worked her way to the front, to stand just behind the railing that was all that was left to separate the sinners from the judgment. Stood there between Sam Sheridan *and Malachi.*

Viola's smile didn't falter, though this wasn't exactly the way she'd wanted things to play out. Best make some lemonade here, then. It was an unexpected piece of good fortune that the Ryan woman was here to see the proceedings, to get an up-close-and-personal view of what happened to folks who didn't sing from Viola Tackett's sheet of music.

What wasn't the good news was that she'd come with Malachi. Viola did very much need to talk to her youngest son, had tried her dead level best to find him so's they could have a sit-down, but he wasn't never where she went looking. Him here like this was not the way she wanted this to play out. Absolutely not. She wanted him to understand what was going on from her perspective, explain to him her plan and his part in it. This was not the best introduction of that plan.

And him here with that Ryan woman and Sam Sheridan. That was not good on so many levels. He'd been spending waaaay too much time with them ever since J-Day. She got it, they'd had a horrible time of it, the three of them together, when Abby Clayton done what she done to that little McClintock girl. Viola knew about that, though most folks in the county — including Abby's people — only knew that she'd had some kinda stroke, went nuts and shot Malachi. They didn't know the kid-in-the-kiln part, and wasn't no reason they needed to. Viola seen how that could make the three of them feel a kinship, going through a thing like that together. And already being friends and all, from when they was kids, even if they hadn't seen each other since high school.

When Malachi started going in to E.J.'s clinic to have his gunshot wound tended, she had dropped the ball, hadn't seen that for what it was, that it was about him spending time with Sam and the other one way more than it was about a bullet wound in the side. But he was a man grown and wasn't up to his mama to tell him how he was supposed to be spending his time. Truth was, ever since J-Day, Malachi had seemed to be getting better. That haunted look in his eyes was fading, he had more expression in his face, didn't seem like he was all the time in some other world and that world was on the other side of hell.

So she was glad for him to be going in to help them as was doing for people got sick from the Jabberwock. If him helping others was helping him, more power to him. She'd missed a step, though, hadn't seen where it was leading, him staying there all the time. Hadn't noticed his ... loyalties, was that the right words — yeah, maybe, his loyalties began to pull away from her and hook up with them two women, E.J. and Liam.

Oh, she knew wasn't no permanent thing. Malachi was a Tackett. He was blood. They wasn't nothing in life more important than blood, than looking out for your own. She knew he'd come down on the side of her and his brothers soon's he found out how she had it all laid out. But she hadn't had a chance to tell him the particulars. Would have given him a heads-up about what was going to happen at the meeting if she coulda found him to tell him.

And now here he was out there on the other side of

that railing separating the world from the law, standing out there on the other side with Sam and the McClintock woman. This wasn't the way it was supposed to go down.

But if Viola Tackett was anything it was a realist. Might not have been ideal, but it was what it was. Malachi'd find out what she was going to do same time everybody else did, and she was sure he'd see through the smoke and mirrors, know she had plans way bigger than just getting rid of one murdering teenager.

Wilbur was still babbling on and on, had done said what he had to say twice and was about to plow that whole row of corn a third time when she stopped him. Rapping her arthritic knuckles on the wooden desktop 'cause she didn't have no gavel, she shut him up in mid repeat.

"That's fine, Mr. Berg. We done heard your whole story twice. Once woulda been plenty. We done here."

She looked out over the crowd that'd gathered. It was a fair-sized group of people, mostly from the Ridge 'cause they could walk to the courthouse and folks was getting choicey about where they went these days, now that it'd dawned on them there wasn't gonna be no gas to fill up they tanks when they ran dry.

Even if they wasn't but a 150 people, every one of them'd tell at least ten other people what they seen and that was plenty.

"I've heard all the testimony I need to hear." She looked at the other two witnesses come to testify — Wilma Thacker, whose raspy voice got on Viola's last nerve, and Ethel Porter. They both looked disappointed they couldn't be part of the show. "I'm ready to give my verdict and pronounce a sentence."

"You mean that's it?" She looked down and seen Holmes Fischer sitting down front. He'd been one of the first people to show up. "Dylan isn't going to be allowed to present a defense?"

"Ain't no reason to waste time with that. I done heard everything that matters."

"But he's got a right to—"

"He ain't got no rights less'n I say he does."

"He's an American citizen and the Bill of Rights—"

"He's a citizen of Nowhere County, Kentucky and the Bill of Rights don't apply here no more. The Jabberwock changed all that and we might not like it but we do got to live with it." She hung a sad look on her face. "'Thout poor Liam to—"

"Liam didn't think Dylan did it."

It was *her*, that McClintock woman, sticking her nose in again where it didn't belong. She was gonna have to learn some manners.

"He told us he didn't," Sam Sheridan said, backing her up. And Sam Sheridan was golden in this county. Wasn't nobody untouchable as far as Viola Tackett was concerned but Sam Sheridan come close as anybody ever would. Even Viola'd bring a world of hurt down on herself if she's to touch so much as a single one of the red hairs on that girl's head. "He came by the clinic after he left Mrs. Whittiker's house and he—"

"Told you somebody besides Dylan Shaw done it? Who?"

"No, he—" said the McClintock woman.

"I thought you said Liam knew who done it."

"That's *not* what I said." Oh, how Viola hated it when somebody took that tone with her. That condescending, I'm-smarter-than-you-are tone. Then she stopped talking to Viola altogether and called out loud so everybody could hear.

"Liam didn't know who did do it. But he said he did know that the murderer *wasn't* Dylan Shaw."

"How'd he come by that conclusion?"

"By investigating the crime scene." Again the condescension, sharper and more intentional, with a side order of sarcasm. "He said Martha Whittiker wasn't killed in that apartment. She was killed somewhere else and the body was moved there. A head wound like hers would have bled a lot and there was hardly any blood on the apartment floor."

"That don't mean—"

The woman interrupted Viola before she had time to finish.

"And he said there was blood … bloody fingerprints on the door of Dylan's apartment."

"You sayin' Liam knowed them fingerprints wasn't Dylan's? Cause that'd be a neat trick seeing's how Liam didn't have no fingerprint kit."

That'd shut her up.

"Liam didn't know whose fingerprints they were, but he found them on the *outside* of the apartment door. If they were Dylan's — say he left them when he was running away — they'd have been on the *inside* of the door. Somebody had blood on their hands going *into the apartment*, not coming out. Why would Dylan kill his grandmother somewhere else and then haul her body back to his own apartment and dump it there?"

If Viola Tackett could have, she'd have leapt up off that seat and ripped that snippy woman's face clean off her head. But she couldn't do that. Not yet, anyway. She would, though. As sure as sunrise on Easter Sunday morning, that McClintock woman was a dead body, up walking around until Viola had time to kill her slow, with her bare hands.

Not now, though. Now, she had to get control of the situation and get on with what she'd come here to do. When Viola spoke again, her words were measured and slow and slathered with menace.

"Liam Montgomery ain't here, and what you *say* he told you ain't admissible in a court of law."

"A court of *law?* Seriously? You call *this* a court of law?"

Viola had had it, and she could tell by the look on Malachi's face that he knew it. He knew his little friend had pushed his mother too far.

She stood up out of the rolled-all-the-way-up chair and leaned over the desk toward the harpy standing next to Malachi.

"It's a court of the only law they is in Nowhere County, Kentucky, so you'd best shut your mouth now, Miss Charlene Ryan McClintock, or I will have one of my boys shut it for you." Malachi stepped protectively in front of her and Viola knew then this was not going to end well.

"*I* am the law in Nowhere County. I'm the judge here and I done heard everything I need to hear." She turned to the sniveling teenager. "You there, Dylan Shaw, I find you guilty of the murder of your grandmother, Martha Whittiker. And I hereby pronounce the death penalty on you for your crime."

In the stunned silence created by the communal gasp that followed, she cut her eyes to her sons and they knew what to do.

"We come prepared for this, done got ourselves a rope." Neb held it up. "We gonna hang you right now from the light pole out front."

Chapter Twenty-Two

MALACHI SHOULD HAVE KNOWN IT. Did know it, actually, but allowed denial to whisper in his ear what he wanted to hear and he'd let things get totally out of hand.

He'd felt a certain detachment as he'd watched his mother presiding over her kangaroo court, with her the judge, the jury ... and the executioners. It was like he was watching somebody else entirely, some woman he barely knew. Not the woman he'd called Mama his whole life.

Oh, it wasn't like his mother had been the warm and fuzzy kind of mother, who kissed his booboos, tucked him into bed every night and told him bedtime stories. He'd once cut his finger so bad you could see the bone, gone running to her and she'd dismissed it with a, "wrap something around that cut, boy, you're dripping blood all over my clean floor."

She'd never been affectionate. Never showed any of his siblings even a hint of maternal tenderness, and as soon as he was old enough to understand, he got it that she was as unable to do that as she was to do quantum physics.

Viola Tackett was a sociopath at the very least, and

much more likely a psychopath. She had not a shred of sympathy or empathy, she traded on fear and intimidation and utter ruthlessness and brooked no disobedience from any of her underlings — which included him, his brothers and sister and all the people who had worked for her over the years.

Yet in a strange, sick kind of way, she did love one of her children. She loved *him*, whatever love meant to a woman of such limited emotional capacity. And maybe Essie, though his older sister was more like a family pet to his mother than a human being. She did care about Malachi, though, and for as long as he could stand it, he tried to please her, to live up to her expectations of him.

The day he had fully understood the extent of her madness, he had left. She had used a sledgehammer to break the kneecaps of a rival doper — made his crew and hers watch. The look in her eyes when she brought the hammer down — that was the last straw. Malachi had gotten into the family's only truck, driven away from Nower County without ever looking back and joined the Marines. Called the Martins who lived at the bottom of Gizzard Ridge and told them to get a message to his mother that her truck was in front of the 4th District Marine Corps recruiting station in Richmond, the keys under the mat.

He didn't go home for two years after that. And when he did go home, he never stayed more than a few days. When he got back to the base after one of his trips home, he took alternating hot and cold showers. It was symbolic. Hot to "wash off the awfulness," and cold to "freeze his responses," to steel himself against the damage to his psyche every second spent in that household wreaked.

Malachi Tackett was way smarter than he had any right to be given his lineage — must have inherited all the

IQ points his siblings had been shorted. Smart enough to avail himself of the services of a herd of military shrinks, most of whom were so blown away by the story of his upbringing they were totally useless. One had been helpful, though — Commander Rubin Kaepernack. He was the man Malachi credited with saving his sanity … until it was shredded in Rwanda.

After Kaepernack listened to Malachi's tales of maternal horror, he had taught Malachi how to survive his brutal upbringing by living his life "based on the wisdom in your scars, not the pain in your wounds." And he cautioned Malachi — *don't ever go home again*. Malachi'd intended to follow his advice. Then Rwanda, and the universe turned his soul wrong side out, and after that, coming home didn't seem any worse than going anywhere else in the world. Because after Rwanda, the trees everywhere dripped blood.

As he watched his mother pronounce a death sentence on an innocent teenager, he understood that his passivity was in part or in whole responsible for what was happening. He'd bowed out, refused to engage and confront, separated himself from Viola Tackett and everything she was about.

But that wasn't good enough. He should have stood up to her, should never have let it get this far. The blood of Liam Montgomery was on his hands and so would the blood of this Shaw kid if he didn't do something.

A BOMB of chaos went off in the courtroom when Viola Tackett sentenced Dylan Shaw to death, but when Sam looked back on it later, she could see that it was controlled chaos. Orchestrated chaos. Much like what happened in the county meeting where she'd murdered Liam Montgomery, Viola Tackett was a couple of steps out ahead of everybody else. She had choreographed the scene, made it her own personal ballet, with everybody in the room unwittingly dancing to her tune.

The natural reaction to the circumstance would have been shocked silence, with a squeak of protest here and there, but certainly not a general unrest. There was, after all, the full force of the whole Tackett clan — sans the youngest son, of course — lined up against them and the explosion of noise and movement, shoving and outcries and general displeasure was surprising. Until it wasn't.

Say you're Viola Tackett and you've set this whole show up for a purpose, as she certainly had done. Would it make a bigger impression to haul the boy out of the courthouse and hang him on the porch steps through a crowd stunned into silence? Or would the bigger, better mousetrap be to haul the boy out through a protesting mob of angry people, a mob Viola would cow, would defy, would stand up against with the brute force of her will, and her sons' guns, of course.

Which story would make the better telling, and exaggerating? That no one had dared make a peep and the boy had been hauled away to his death against no opposition whatsoever? Or that there was outrage — defiance and opposition that Viola Tackett stomped into submission, clearly demonstrating that she was stronger and more powerful than the combined opposition of a room full of outraged citizens?

The yelling had erupted in an instant, volcanic blast. And as in the meeting where Viola had gunned down her only legal opposition, it came from everywhere in the room at once. From people Viola had planted. Stooges whose job it was to stir up the emotion of the folks around them.

People like Ethel Porter and Wilma Thacker, Martha Whittiker's neighbors who hadn't taken a whole lot of convincing to believe their lives were in mortal danger every second the druggie grandmother-killer was at large.

Buddy and Mary Jo Cawdrey, who lived on Bump Road in the north end of the county on the bank of the Rolling Fork and whose loyalty was for sale to whoever had the best weed.

Burt Donaldson from Poorfolk, and Jeb Pruitt, Clyde Biggerstaff and Milt Watson from Killarney — all Viola's neighbors.

Even ditzy Sally Ann McMurtry, the still-lost-in-the-60s hippie chic who opposed violence in any form, up to and including shooting a deer to put food on the table.

At the most dramatic moment, Viola would swoop in and squash all opposition under her jackbooted authority in a grand show of domination.

Malachi's brother Obie, the second oldest of Viola's sons, had been standing with Dylan when Sam, Charlie and Malachi had come rushing into the courtroom to find the boy babbling and blubbering while Viola listened in stony silence. The other brothers were not immediately in evidence until Neb stepped out of the crowd to the left at his mother's signal and held up a heavy rope dangling a hangman's noose. Zach stepped out of the crowd on the right and the three converged on Dylan, surrounding him, giving him a quick bum's rush toward the door. There were other obvious plants in the crowd who'd been instructed to impede the progress of anybody who might be legitimately and sincerely inclined to step forward in the boy's defense. It was all a grand concert, everybody playing from Viola's sheet of music, louder and softer at the direction of the maestro.

The first person and the most vocal and hard to

control, was Fish. Surprisingly, Holmes Fischer went off like a bottle rocket when Viola had rapped her knuckles on the desk and nodded for Dylan to be led from the courtroom to his death.

He'd been sitting on the floor in front, looking worse than usual, but he had been deteriorating markedly ever since J-Day, courtesy of an ever-shrinking supply of the alcohol that coursed through his veins to lubricate and soothe his jangled nerves and stave off the DT's.

She'd have thought the man couldn't have gotten any skinnier. How could you be more thin than skin stretched taught over a skeleton? But he had shrunk, somehow, and looked pitifully haggard and hollow-eyed.

For a homeless man who wasn't, by its strictest definition, homeless, Holmes Fischer had always hung onto his self-respect. There was some semblance of dignified aplomb to his carriage, a subtle message that he had not always been as he appeared now, that he once had been more than just an upstanding member of society. He'd been on the upper tier, an educated man in a county where ninety percent of the residents couldn't read above an eighth-grade level. An erudite scholar.

A shadow of that had remained as he sank into alcoholism, and he seemed able to summon it occasionally, slip into it like draping a cloak over his shoulders to cover his deficiencies so he could operate on a level with other sober people.

There was none of that left in him now. He was a desperately skinny drunk, with cigarette-burn holes in his face for eyes and an unkempt, unshaven look that even a decade of semi-homelessness had not produced.

When Viola spoke, he leapt to his feet, staggering, and cried out, "No, you can't do that. No!"

He sounded almost hysterical, and it was clear from the

look Viola gave him that she hadn't planned that particular outburst and hadn't gotten troops in place to deal with it, quash it before it had a chance to light a flame of genuine resistance.

Her choreography hadn't anticipated Malachi's presence either, and though he was not loud and attention-gathering like Fish, he was infinitely more dangerous.

Malachi turned toward Dylan, clearly intent on getting to him before his brothers had a chance, and spiriting him away.

His two oldest brothers, Neb and Obie, were closer to the boy than Malachi and had pulled their weapons on the noisy crowd. Malachi ignored their guns and charged toward them, and they were clearly unprepared for the presence of somebody they absolutely could *not* shoot, not even in self-defense.

Zach came up behind Malachi and tried to grab him, but Malachi spun on him, hammered him with a quick jab to the face he totally wasn't expecting and wasn't prepared for and he crashed backward onto the floor.

Whenever Sam recalled what happened after that, she could never fit the circumstances into the time it took for them to occur.

Obie held Dylan by the upper arm, Neb stood on the other side of the boy with a gun in one hand and a hangman's rope in the other. Malachi stopped a few steps from the three of them. He drew the pistol out of the holster at his side, the gun he'd produced out of the duffel bag he'd brought when he "moved into" E.J.'s apartment above the clinic. He didn't point it at anybody, just held it loosely in front of him. Even in the orchestrated cacophony of the room, Sam could hear what Malachi said to them.

"Put the guns away, you idiots. You aren't going to shoot me or anybody else. Let him go."

They stood defiantly in place. Neb might have flicked a quick look toward Sam and Charlie but he snapped his eyes back toward Malachi and stood his ground.

"Mind your own business, Mal, this ain't none of your con—"

"Stand down." The menace in Malachi's voice was thick enough to spread on toast. "Do it now before I have to hurt you. And I *will* hurt you."

He still didn't raise the gun toward his brothers and it was clear whatever he did to them, he could, if he chose, do with his bare hands.

That was when Sam felt her presence. There was no possible way Viola could have gotten up from her seat behind the big desk on the platform and crossed the open area inside the railing to where she and Charlie were standing in the time it took Malachi to confront his brothers.

But she had.

Sam spotted her out of the corner of her eye and was so surprised she actually leapt back. Charlie didn't leap back, though. She couldn't. Viola had an iron grip on her upper arm with one hand and a pistol jammed into her side with the other.

"Only person's gonna get hurt here, son, is yore little friend," she said, and he whirled toward where she had the drop on Charlie. "You 'stand down,' or I will blast a hole in her big enough to drive a forklift through."

Chapter Twenty-Three

CHARLIE DIDN'T SEE Viola's approach, but she did smell her coming. The old woman had an earthy aroma that was part the smell of damp ground in a garden and part the smell of clothes that'd been worn so often no amount of laundry detergent would ever get them completely clean, an old-fabric smell that reminded Charlie of thrift store clothing. She'd noticed it the day they'd all piled into E.J.'s van for the ride out to the county line for their first look at the mirror-in-the-road Jabberwock.

By the time she actually saw Viola, it was too late to do anything but submit to the iron grip on her upper arm and the feel of the gun barrel in her side.

Viola was squeezing her arm tighter than she needed just to restrain her, and Charlie could feel the rage flowing down through her into her grip, knew if she could have pinched Charlie's arm off above the elbow she'd had done it in a heartbeat.

And Charlie made a show of trying to shake off the grip, not that she believed for a moment she could free herself, but in defiance. In principle. She wouldn't just stand there like a cigar store Indian and allow the dumpy little dictator to yank her around.

Viola shot her a glance when she did, a look of desolate hatred that was stunning in its ferocity. It wasn't until that moment that a couple of things occurred to Charlie. One, Viola Tackett was not accustomed to anybody standing up to her. She was used to giving orders and then standing by while all her minions scurried around to do her bidding. Charlie was granting the woman a brand new experience.

And two, Viola Tackett would be more than happy to kill her, put a bullet in her right on the spot, shoot her down without provocation just like she had Liam. Only two things restrained her from that violent impulse. The crowd of onlookers. And Malachi.

"Let her go, Mama." The edge of menace in his voice was every bit as lethal as the tone of his mother's. Though they were certainly not moral equals, neither had a will stronger than the other. Malachi Tackett had never been more his mother's son than at that moment.

"Step aside and let us get on with bidness that don't concern you."

"He's just a kid what — sixteen or seventeen? You can't just string him up."

"Can and will. You need to step out of the way.

The faux chaos and fabricated opposition Viola had worked so hard to orchestrate had died away out of the crowd. No one spoke now, or made any move — either toward Dylan or away from him. They all stood in silence, watching the mother/son drama play out on the stage before them.

Instead of moving out of the way, Malachi took a step that put him between Dylan Shaw and his mother.

"You want him, you're going to have to shoot me."

"Now you know I ain't going to do that, Malachi." Her voice almost sounded maternal. Almost. Then she cocked the pistol. "But I will shoot this butt-in-ski little shrew here, drop her with a single bullet right to the heart." She paused, looked him dead in the eye. "You know I ain't bluffing, boy. You seen enough in all the years you was eating at my table to know I mean ever word I say."

Charlie looked from one to the other of them, knowing that both of them would die before they'd back down.

Zach began to stagger to his feet, wiping the blood from his split lip on the back of his hand, and Malachi shot a glance his way. Neb struck like a rattlesnake. Maybe there'd been a signal from his mother, but Charlie didn't think so. He had just seized the opportunity that presented itself, Malachi's inattention for the second's advantage he needed. Taking a single step forward, he slammed the barrel of his pistol into the back of his younger brother's head with a force that pulled a squeak of a scream from Sam's throat.

Malachi dropped to the floor, his own pistol under his limp body.

There was a one-beat pause, a second of elongated silence during which Charlie felt her own life hanging by a thread. There was absolutely nothing to stop Viola Tackett from shooting her. No reason for the little woman not to set loose the rage Charlie could feel in the clawed fingers of her hand.

She felt the gun barrel jab harder into her side and closed her eyes, wondering what would happen to Merrie now, who would look after her.

"I ain't done with you, Missy." The words rode a whisper of bad breath into Charlie's face. "You will die at my hand, know that for the absolute truth that it is. I ain't never in my life broke a promise." The old woman looked around. "Right now ain't the time, though, so I'll give you the gift of another couple of sunrises 'fore I *cut you down*."

She shoved Charlie violently at Sam, who stumbled from the impact and the two of them almost landed on the floor beside Malachi.

"Handcuff him," Viola told Obie, nodding toward the lump of unconscious Malachi on the floor. Then she wagged her pistol in the direction of the utterly terrified Dylan Shaw. "We done wasted enough time already."

Her words snapped the gawking crowd out of its trance, but the pandemonium atmosphere she had obviously intended to accompany the act was hopelessly gone and there was nothing Viola could have done to resurrect it.

The crowd was as mute as a eunuch. The only sounds were the shuffling of feet and the mewling cries of the terrified teenager who was beginning to realize he had only minutes to live.

"Come on, now, let's git 'er done," Viola said and lead a reluctant parade out of the room, as Sam and Charlie knelt beside the unconscious form of Malachi on the floor.

Chapter Twenty-Four

No.

No, no, no, no!

This couldn't be, wasn't happening. It was all wrong, so wrong!

Fish had to do something!

But what? What could Fish do even sober? And he was far from sober. Not far enough, though, and that was the problem. Ever since J-Day, he had been unable to get drunk enough so that what happened didn't matter, so life flowed past him on the breeze with a gentle buzzing sound behind it, framed sometimes in an almost golden glow.

He hadn't seen the golden glow or heard the buzzing sound since he woke up in the Dollar General Store parking lot two weeks ago, choking to death on his own tongue. Wasn't for lack of effort on his part. He had done nothing else since that day but seek out the alcohol he needed in sufficient quantities to blot out the world. He had always been able to manage that before. Now, the law of supply and demand had changed all that in the blink of an eye.

Finite amount of booze. Infinite need for it. Problem.

That's what he'd been doing at Martha Whittiker's place. Dear holy mother of God he had never meant to harm anyone! Never would have dreamed of doing such a thing. He had waited until he knew she wouldn't be home to sneak into her house and raid her supply of alcoholic beverages. But she had come home sooner than he'd expected. And somehow — even now, more sober than he had been in years, he could not remember exactly what happened. She had walked in on him as he clutched a bottle of Maker's Mark whiskey to his bosom and the next thing he knew she was lying on the floor in a puddle of blood and he was running away as fast as he could.

But he'd gone back! Later, he'd gone back to make sure the poor old lady wasn't hurt badly, to apologize profusely and beg her forgiveness, to grovel and to return the booze he had stolen — even the bottle of Maker's.

Instead of the poor old lady with a knot on her head and a bee in her bonnet he had found a dead body. He had killed Martha Whittiker. He'd moved the body, put it in Dylan Shaw's apartment out back so the boy would be blamed for the crime *only* because he knew the kid would not suffer any consequences. He was only a boy, for crying out loud, barely old enough for a driver's license. Sure, he was a drug-addicted, drug dealer "lowlife," but he was still just a kid and Fish would never have considered getting him blamed for a murder if he hadn't been completely certain that the boy's youth would get him off.

Nobody'd harm a kid!

And by the time the Jabberwock finally let go its grip on the county and the law showed up to investigate the murder, there'd be no evidence left to connect anybody to the crime — the real doer, Fish, or his patsy, Dylan Shaw.

As Fish sat helplessly by and watched Viola Tackett try,

convict and sentence the boy to death, he could think of nothing he could do to stop her, to save the kid.

Except confess.

The only way to convince anybody that Dylan Shaw hadn't killed his grandmother was to admit that he, Holmes Fischer, had done the deed.

So he tried. He tried to stand and protest, tried to get Viola Tackett to listen to reason — and then the world went mad and the next thing he knew he was staggering along at the end of a line of people moving with purpose down the courthouse hallway and the wide stairs to the first floor and out the front doors of the building onto the wide porch. Standing sentinel on both sides of the porch were light poles, each with arms that extended out to hold an ornate lantern-shaped light over the steps.

The lights in those lanterns hadn't burned in a decade. Unlike the ones on the pole in the Middle of Nowhere, nobody had been civic-minded enough to replace the bulbs in these. Useless as light fixtures, they'd nonetheless make a dandy hangman's tree.

And by the time Fish had stumbled out the doorway behind the crowd, Neb had thrown a rope with a noose tied on the end over the extension arm on the pole on the right and had set up a ladder beneath it.

Lurching forward, Fish cried out into the strange, unearthly silence that wafted up off the crowd of onlookers like stink off a stagnant pool.

"Don't. Wait. He didn't kill her."

His words were slurred and no one paid him any attention. When Viola Tackett stepped past him, Fish reached out and grabbed her by the arm, withstood her frightening stare of disapproval and told her in an earnest voice.

"You have to let him go. It wasn't him!"

The sincerity in his voice persuaded her as no words

could have and she paused and gave him a moment of her attention. He had just that one moment, that heartbeat of time, to stop the murder of an innocent boy.

"I did it, Viola. It was me. I didn't mean to. As God is my witness, it was an accident. I was stealing liquor when she came in—"

He watched understanding dawn in her eyes, followed quickly though reluctantly with belief. She yanked him aside and spoke in a harsh whisper.

"You saying it was *you* killed Martha Whittiker?"

"I put her body in his place so he'd be blamed. I knew nobody'd do anything about it because he's just a kid. You can't hang him for a crime he didn't commit." He paused before he continued, and realized as he said the words how freeing they were. He'd been struggling for so many years, running from the memories of that night, of that encounter with the minions of the pit of hell. Now, he wouldn't have to struggle anymore. Now he could end it. Though he'd considered it a thousand times, he'd never had the guts to commit suicide. Now somebody else would do that part for him.

"Hang me. I'm the guilty one."

She looked at him and he watched a range of emotions chase each other across her face. She was thinking, calculating, planning.

"You telling me I'd ought to hang you for what you done, is that what you're telling me?"

He swallowed. "Yes, that's what I'm telling you."

"So you deserve to die, which means if I let you off, you owe me your life — that's the way of it — right?"

He didn't know where she might be going with this and then he realized she was going to grant him clemency, that she believed he never intended to hurt Martha Whittiker, that it'd been an accident.

Relief flowed over him in a warm flood. He wasn't going to die here after all.

"Yes, Viola. *I owe you my life.*"

"We gonna talk about what that means, you and me, later, when I got the time."

Of course, she had to tell the crowd eager for blood that there would be no public execution here this afternoon. They could all go home.

Viola pushed him aside and stepped out onto the edge of the porch. The crowd of people had assembled on the steps below where they could look up and see the terrified Shaw kid, hands tied behind him, standing on the ladder. Neb had slipped the noose around the kid's neck and Zach was pushing him up the steps while Neb pulled on the rope to force him to keep moving.

"Listen up, everybody," she said, in a voice to be heard above a noisy crowd. Except this one was dead silent. "I just found out something you all need to hear."

She gestured to where Fish stood, leaned for balance against the courthouse wall. "I know some of you's been concerned we got the wrong man here, after listening to the blathering of that woman, saying Liam didn't believe Dylan here done it. So's you's feeling bad, thinking maybe we was about to execute an innocent man. Well, Fish here done stepped forward and cast away all the doubt. He knows who it was killed that poor old woman — doncha, Fish?"

The crowd turned toward him and he nodded his head.

"Fish was there, in Martha Whittiker's house. He was *stealing* a bottle of whiskey so he was scared to come forward and say so. But now that he's finally admitted the truth, we can all rest in our souls that justice is being done here today."

For the first time since he'd looked down at the bleeding body of that poor old woman on the floor in front of him, Fish knew that everything really was going to be alright.

Then Viola turned and stepped toward the ladder where the boy was now balanced on the top step on his tiptoes. Fish noticed when she did so that the rope was already cutting into the kid's neck and that the front of his pants were stained dark where he'd wet himself.

"Dylan Shaw, you got any last words?"

Fish's eyes snapped from Dylan to Viola. He must have heard her wrong. Why would …?

"I figured not. You gonna send out a message loud and clear to everybody in Nowhere County — they'd best toe the straight and narrow or Viola Tackett will see they get what they deserve!"

And with that she gave a mighty shove and the ladder fell out from under the boy.

He was looking right at Fish. In his last instant of life on earth, Dylan Shaw's eyes had locked with Fish's.

Then his head snapped sideways and he went limp, swaying slowly back and forth beneath the light pole on the courthouse steps.

Chapter Twenty-Five

TOBY WITHERSPOON COULDN'T SEE a thing from where he was standing. There were too many grownups in front of him and they weren't about to move so a little boy could squeeze his way to the front and watch a hanging. If they noticed him, they'd ask if his mother knew he was here and tell him to go home.

He had waited until his father was bleary-eyed drunk, then he had pulled the dirty purse wrapped up in a towel out from under his bed and put it in a garbage bag to take downtown and show the sheriff. He didn't have one of those dumb girls' bikes he saw sometimes on old television shows that had a basket on the front, though he secretly thought a basket on the front would be a handy thing to have on a bike.

His was a 10-speed, though, a big one so tall he had to lean it over with his foot on the ground when he straddled the bar. Ten-speeds weren't designed for dumb girl things like baskets, so he had wrapped the garbage bag that contained his mother's purse around and around his waist and tied it tight with the pull ties so it wouldn't fall off. Then he had set out for town.

Only eight years old, Toby Witherspoon had never actually ridden his bike all the way into town from his house on Iron Rock Road. He had ridden the distance a hundred dozen times in the car, though, so he knew the way and how long it was, knew he could surely ride his bike that far.

But as he pumped hard on the pedals up the hills and rode the brake down the other side on the shoulder of the road, he broke into a sweat, his breath heaving in and out.

It wasn't a hot day. Just like every day since J-Day, there wasn't a cloud in the sky — which didn't seem right to Toby but he was just a kid so what did he know? He was drenched in sweat and it had taken him three times as long as he'd thought it would, but he had finally made it into town and was cruising down Main Street toward the court-house when a bunch of people came pouring out the front door of the building. He pulled his bike over onto the side-walk, got off and leaned it against the big concrete planter that grew nothing but weeds now. He tried to get close enough to see what was going on but it was hopeless.

He did get close enough to hear the murmured conver-sations of the adults who were standing there explaining what was going on to some newcomers. Some teenager had killed his grandmother. There'd been a trial and he'd been convicted … and they were about to hang him right there on the courthouse steps.

Toby was staggered by the news.

"Viola Tackett's the law now, alright. Don't need no jury trial."

"Don't need no evidence, neither. She just listened to what Wilbur said he seen and the next thing you know …" He didn't finish, just gestured like he had a rope in his hand that was tied around his neck. He pulled on the imaginary rope and made a face like he was choking.

Toby stood in shocked disbelief.

Didn't need any evidence? This Viola Tackett person, who must be the sheriff or the judge or something like that now, just listened to what people said and *believed* them.

Toby didn't have to find his mother's body — though he was sure now that when he told them where the dog'd dug up her purse, they would dig there and find it. All he needed was to get to this Viola Tackett person and tell her his story. Then she'd go out and arrest his father and they'd hang him from the courthouse steps.

Toby had to see this.

Then he remembered the Bible story he'd learned in Vacation Bible School, when his teacher had been that fat girl who was the preacher's daughter. Hayley was her name. He remembered her because she had been real nice to him until he'd let it slip about his mother. He'd said he didn't believe in prayer because he had asked God over and over to keep his father from hurting his mother but God hadn't stopped him. And after that, Hayley looked at him funny and didn't smile at him anymore.

But she had taught them a Bible story about a "wee little man" named Zacchaeus, who had wanted to see Jesus, but he was so short he couldn't see over the taller people in front of him. So he had climbed up in a tree to see.

That's what Toby Witherspoon did.

There weren't any trees right next to the courthouse, but a small maple was growing in one of those special tree holes they made sometimes in the sidewalk and in the concrete around buildings. It was a smallish tree, but that was really the good news because it wouldn't have held anybody bigger than Toby.

It took him several tries before he was able to scramble up the skinny trunk and grab hold of the lowest-hanging limb. Then he pulled himself up to his waist, threw his leg over the limb and sat straddling it, which put him just a little over the height of the people standing between him and the courthouse steps.

What he saw there made him instantly sick to his stomach.

There was a ladder with a kid on it who didn't look to be a whole lot older than Toby. He was standing on tiptoes on the top step, with his hands bound behind his back and a rope in a noose around his neck. Some lady stepped forward then. The woman was short and dumpy and ugly. An old lady with crooked teeth and a big bun of dark hair sitting on the back of her neck.

That must be Viola Tackett, the woman the man'd been talking about, the one who listened to the evidence and decided whether somebody was guilty or not.

She called out to the crowd, said something about a fish that had made it clear the kid on the ladder really had killed his grandmother — something like that. Then she'd turned her face up toward the kid — and it looked like he had peed his pants, since the front of his jeans was a dark blue. She asked him if he had any last words, and when he didn't say anything she stepped back and shoved the ladder over!

Just shoved it over. Toby looked away, felt bile rising up in the back of his throat, and only glanced out of the corner of his eye at the kid — the kid's *body*, he was dead — hanging there by the neck, his head twisted at an impossible angle on his shoulders.

Viola Tackett. That was the woman's name. That's who Toby had to see to tell her about how his father had killed his mother.

Chapter Twenty-Six

SAM AND CHARLIE knelt beside the unconscious Malachi, and Charlie felt a profound sense of deja vu all over again, harking back to kneeling on the floor beside Liam after Viola shot him in the back. Killed him. Without a shred of care or remorse. And she was about to hang that poor Shaw kid without any more feeling than she'd had for Liam.

It was beginning to dawn on Charlie that Viola Tackett was a woman everybody in the world underestimated, and lived to regret it. If they lived long enough to tell the tale.

Clearly, Viola had been planning to kill Liam from the git-go; it was no crime of opportunity. It was part and parcel of her overall scheme to take over Nower County that she'd probably started planning on J-Day. So far, it appeared to be chugging down the track with a full head of steam right on schedule.

She didn't think any of it surprised Malachi.

He had looked grim when Raylynn told them what his mother was doing, that she was sitting as judge and jury for the kid Liam had said didn't kill his grandmother.

"Yeah, it figures that's where she'd go next." But he hadn't elaborated and neither she nor Sam was inclined to question him about it.

It was obvious now that he understood there was going to be no effort to determine if the kid was innocent or guilty, that his mother was using the kid just as she had used Liam, stepping over their bodies on her climb to the top of the heap. Though Charlie wasn't completely sure she understood the reasoning, she'd bet it had something to do with demonstrating her power, to cow those who might dare to oppose her.

Which of course, lead to the inescapable conclusion that Viola Tackett absolutely would have killed Charlie if it had happened to work into her current plans. And that she *would* kill Charlie, just as soon as she got around to it.

"You need … to get out of here," Malachi said, and she hadn't even realized he had regained consciousness. Coming around as fast as he did seemed to indicate that he hadn't been knocked completely out, which made sense given that the blow came from his own brother, who likely didn't give a rip about Malachi but did know that his butt would be in a crack if he happened to accidentally harm Mama's favorite little boy.

Malachi was lying on his back with his hands hand-cuffed behind him.

"Now, right now. Leave."

She didn't have to ask why.

"Help me get him up," she said to Sam.

"No, leave me. Go on — while she's still occupied."

"We're not leaving you here to—"

"Mama wouldn't hurt me. I'm not in any danger." He turned his eyes on Charlie. "But *you* are."

"She threatened to kill me." Charlie hadn't meant to reveal what Viola'd whispered in her face; it'd just slipped out. Sam gasped but Malachi didn't seem the least surprised.

"You have to get away from here before she gets finished out there and turns her attention on you." He looked at Sam. "Get her out of here! Stick her somewhere she won't be seen for a while."

Charlie knew there wasn't anywhere she could hide in Nowhere County that Viola Tackett couldn't find her. "What good will that—?"

"I've got to talk her off the ledge," he said. "Bargain with her. Make a deal."

"A deal to keep her from killing Charlie? What—?" Sam said.

"Maybe I can convince her I've seen the light, that blood's thicker than water ... some kind of crap like that. *I* am my only bargaining chip. She wants me on her side and she might be willing to trade that for" — he looked Charlie in the eye, his gaze frigid — "your life."

They could hear Viola's voice, shouting at the crowd from the steps, but it wasn't loud enough to hear what she was saying. The crowd's sudden reaction carried clearly, though. Women screamed, a couple of them, and there was some kind of communal gasp and groan, a visceral response to watching somebody die right before their eyes.

"Out the back door, down the back steps," Malachi ordered.

"But—"

"Go *now!*"

Sam grabbed Charlie's arm and literally yanked her to her feet, then headed toward the doorway that lead out the back side of the courtroom. Either Sam knew where she was going or she had just guessed right because the door led into an anteroom, apparently where the judge got dressed up in a robe, then into an office that was empty except for a single rolling chair sitting in the middle of the room, and out the door of that office that opened on the second-floor hallway. The back stairs lay on the other side of a closed door and they hurried down them to the first floor, where Sam stopped and opened the door a crack and peeked out. There were people at the far end of the hallway coming back in the front doors. Sam suddenly shoved the door shut.

"Viola!" she whispered and the two of them froze.

They waited a few seconds, then Sam eased the door open a crack again. "She's going upstairs."

As soon as Sam saw Viola and the other boys turn the corner on the first-floor landing and start up the stairs to the second floor, she threw the door open and sprinted across the back of the hallway and out the back door of the building. Under normal circumstances, Charlie would have had trouble keeping up with the fleet-footed former basketball player. Terror fueled her now and she matched Sam step for step.

At the corner of the building outside, they paused, then walked slowly into the crowd that was milling around the steps, past a tree where a little boy was climbing down the trunk. He was just a little boy, maybe eight years old, and he'd climbed up in that tree so he could see the hanging. He'd watched!

The boy darted away into the crowd and Charlie kept her head turned, refused to look in the direction of the courthouse steps, where she knew somebody was at that moment hauling down the dead body of a teenage boy murdered by Viola Tackett.

Chapter Twenty-Seven

MALACHI WAS SITTING UP, leaned against the railing in the courtroom with his pistol in his lap when his mother and brothers came back into the room. She came directly to him, stood over him, looking down.

"You alright?"

"What do you care? I'm not dripping blood on your clean kitchen floor."

She offered a crooked smile at that.

"Take them cuffs off," she told Obie, and Malachi watched a stricken look appear on his brother's face as he began to frantically pat his pockets. "You lose that key and I'll—"

"I got it, Ma," he said, holding it forth like a kid that'd just pulled his first tooth. And Malachi was struck anew by how unutterably dumb his brothers were. Zach had a little on the ball, but you could combine the IQs of Neb and Obie and still not get a two-digit number.

Obie knelt and Malachi turned to offer his hands so Obie could unlock the cuffs when a little boy burst into the room, looking around frantically.

"Get that kid outta here," Viola told Neb, but as soon as she spoke the kid made a beeline for her. He was a rail-thin boy with blond hair falling in his eyes and a lower lip that stuck out a little like a natural pout.

"Are you Vio-da Pickett?"

She didn't answer, just gestured toward the door and Neb stepped forward and grabbed the kid by the arm to drag him out.

"No, wait. They said you was the judge and jury," he cried, pulling frantically away. "There ain't no law but you. You gotta help me."

"Get him outta here."

"No, please. You don't understand." Neb began dragging the struggling child toward the door. "My daddy murdered my mama."

Neb stopped dragging and looked at Viola.

"What are you talking about, son?" she asked.

Neb let go of the boy and the kid ran up to Viola and started babbling, while Malachi got to his feet, rubbing his wrists where the handcuffs had chafed. He didn't touch the throbbing knot on the back of his head, though. Didn't want to set it off to pounding again. He leaned over and picked up his pistol off the floor.

"He beat her up all the time and hurt her with the belt but the ladies in her Bunco didn't know because he made sure the bruises were where they couldn't see."

That appeared to pique Viola's interest because it had the ring of truth. A kid his age wouldn't know a thing like that unless he'd actually seen it.

"And he hurt her all the time and it was really bad and I saw her the morning of J-Day in the kitchen and they were yelling and I ran off because it scared me and at Billy's house they were talking about the Jabberwock and his mama wanted to go see and so she took us to the

Middle of Nowhere and we looked. It stunk, everybody was puking and then she took me home and Daddy was there but Mama wasn't and when I asked where she was he said it wasn't any of my business. She didn't come home that night — she never doesn't come home! The next day, Daddy heard about the Jabberwock and he told everybody that Mama had left the day before to go see her sister in Lexington — but she *didn't.* I *saw* her. And last night he came home with blood all over him and his face all mashed in and I knew he had been in a fight and maybe hurt somebody else and I went looking for proof, you know, evidence, like Detective Sipowicz woulda done—"

"Stop!" his mother held up her hand, clearly out of patience. "What makes you think your daddy—?"

"I got evidence! Proof. Custard was Mama's dog and she got off the leash this morning and ran away and when she came back, she was carrying my mama's purse." Malachi noticed for the first time that the boy was carrying something wrapped in a garbage bag. "Here," he said and began unwrapping the package. He took out of it a dirt-encrusted purse and held it out to Viola. "See. Custard dug it up. It's my mama's purse."

Viola didn't take the purse, just looked at the kid.

"Mama wouldn't have left town without her purse."

Now, Malachi was more than a little interested. The kid was right. No woman he'd ever met would allow herself to be separated from her purse for more than ten minutes. Certainly wouldn't have gone out of town and left it behind.

And somebody'd buried the purse, had tried to hide it. Though his mother's face was a mask of disinterest, Malachi knew she was thinking the same thing.

When Viola still said nothing, the boy opened the purse and dumped out the contents on the floor. There was a wallet, a plastic zipped bag that probably carried makeup, pieces of gum, receipts, a blue plastic thing, hair ties, a pen and a pair of glasses and other miscellaneous trash. The boy picked up the blue plastic thing.

"Mama has asthma," he said. "She never goes anywhere without her inhaler. She can't breathe." He dropped the inhaler, picked up the billfold and held it out to Viola.

"Look in this."

Viola took the wallet and opened it up, examined it as he continued his desperate monologue. "See. See! Her driver's license is in there. She wouldn't have left town without her driver's license. And her credit cards. Daddy said she went shopping with her sister in Lexington but how could she go shopping without any credit cards?"

The kid was right, of course. Malachi knew it and so did his mother.

"I think I know where Custard dug up the purse but I'm not sure because I didn't want to go there."

The kid had been barreling along, his emotions carrying him full speed ahead but now those same emotions clogged his throat and he had trouble talking.

"I helped Mama dig the pit for the compost heap. It's deep. If that's where Custard dug up her purse, then maybe …"

He couldn't go on. Had been propelled by his fear and anger but now the emotion was grief and it was too big and heavy for the kid to carry.

"You think yore daddy kilt yore mama and buried her and her purse in the compost heap — that what you's telling me?"

The boy wasn't crying and Malachi was proud of him for it. He was swallowing hard to keep from it, though he couldn't control the wash of tears that poured down his cheeks. He nodded his head slowly, his lip trembling.

"Yes, ma'am," he said, surprising Malachi that he was able to pull the words out of his throat.

"What's your name, kid?"

"Toby Witherspoon."

"Howie Witherspoon's boy? Your daddy owns the Dollar General Store, don't he?"

He nodded.

She turned to Neb. "Take this kid into that office." To the boy she said, "You wait there till I tell you to come out, hear?"

He nodded and Neb led him away. To Zach, she said, "Call Howie. Tell him I want to talk to him, to haul his goat-smellin' butt down to the courthouse right now — he don't live far. If he ain't home or at the store, go find him."

Zach went off to make the call and Viola was finally able to direct her full attention to Malachi.

"You wanna tell me what you was doing in here this morning with that woman and Sam Sheridan?"

"No."

"What do you mean no?"

"How many things can no mean? No, I won't tell you what I was doing this morning or any other morning or explain to you who I was with and why that was. I'm a grown man, Mama, and unlike my idiot brothers, I have enough real estate between my ears that I don't need my mother to make my decisions for me."

"You done? Was that all the speech you wanted to make?"

"You don't want to hear the speech I'd really like to make."

"What, you think you tell me the truth you gonna hurt my feelings?"

"That would assume you have feelings to hurt, Mama, and you don't."

"Meaning?"

"Meaning you are a heartless, self-centered sociopath who will stop at nothing to get what she wants."

"That about covers it."

"Up to and including committing cold-blooded murder."

"Uh huh, including murder. And you're the only mother's child on this planet could say a thing like that to me 'thout me provin' the truth of it by putting a bullet 'tween their eyes."

"You won't shoot me, Mama."

"No, I won't." She paused, looked him up and down, and he could hear the words coming before she opened her mouth. "But I will shoot that little friend of yours, what's her name, Sylvia Ryan's youngest?"

"Her name is Charlie McClintock. And if you—"

"If I *what*, you'll *what?*" she snapped at him, eyes flashing. "This here's what they call a Mexican standoff. You know I ain't gonna shoot you and I know you ain't gonna shoot me."

"I wouldn't count on that." He looked down at the gun in his own hand, but it wasn't a bluff he could run. That was the thing. She had him and she knew it. She was his mother. He couldn't threaten to kill her because they both knew he wasn't capable of the kind of indiscriminate violence she served up whenever it suited her. He couldn't shoot her down in cold blood. But she could and absolutely would do that to Charlie.

He stuffed the pistol into the waistband of his jeans in the back and let his tee shirt drop over it.

"What do you want from me, Mama?" His voice was as hard and cold as an Arctic glacier.

"For you to do right by your family, that's what. You's kin. We're blood. Ain't nothing in life important as that and you need to own up to your responsibilities."

"Meaning?"

"Don't cross me, boy. Don't you set yourself up on the other side of what I'm doing. This here is *my* county and I'm gonna run it as suits me and ain't nobody … *nobody* gonna get in my way and live to see another sunrise."

"If you think I'm going to help you—"

"You hear me asking for your help? I'm doing just fine my own self, thank you very much, and I don't need nothing from you nor nobody else." She paused for a beat. "But I will not tolerate one of mine lining up against me. You understand what I'm saying, boy?"

"And if I stay out of it …?"

"Your little friend — what's her name? Charlie? That ain't no proper name for a girl. She'll keep breathing in and out on a regular basis for a right smart while yet, 'til she runs afoul of somebody meaner'n me who won't tolerate that lip she's got on her."

He said nothing, just looked at her.

She returned his glare, then her stony stare softened about half a degree.

"Fair 'nough," she said and nodded.

She looked like she might even have been going to reach out to Malachi — oh, nothing so effusive as a hug. As far back as Malachi could recall, he'd never seen his mother hug anybody. A hand on his arm, though, maybe or—

Before she could move, a disheveled man rushed breathless into the courtroom. He looked like he'd been kicked in the face by a mule. His nose was smashed over onto his cheek, both eyes were black, his lip was busted, one of his front teeth was broken and there were four long scratches slicing down the whole length of his left cheek — the kinds of scratches made by a woman's fingernails.

His left hand was crudely bandaged, gauze wrapped around his thumb.

Howie Witherspoon. The man who had killed Toby's mother.

Chapter Twenty-Eight

STUART RODE in the front seat of Jolene's van as they headed down Route 17 south from the Middle of Nowhere. Cotton had given her Reece's address, said it was the other side of Bennettville, but Jolene turned off almost immediately on Gallagher Station Road and Stuart was reluctant to point out that Cotton hadn't gone this way. She must have noticed his discomfiture because she smiled.

"Cotton turned on Cicada Springs Road, didn't he, farther down? There are half a dozen different ways to get from point A to point B in the mountains. Everybody has their own preference."

They were silent then for a few minutes and Stuart found tension winding tighter with every mile, dread settling around him like ash out of the air after the eruption of a volcano.

"Why do you call it, whatever it is, the Jabberwock?" she asked.

"Because that's what Shep Clayton called it and it appeared to me that maybe he'd actually met the gentleman."

He told her the story of Shep and his newborn son, coming home to a hundred-year-old shack.

"Cotton and I went to visit him yesterday and he definitely doesn't have both oars in the water. He said the 'Jabberwock' didn't want us here, that it didn't like for people to meddle in its affairs. That we should leave."

"You don't think he made it all up because he's crazy, not that I wouldn't be crazy if I were him."

"Maybe. Maybe not." Stuart paused. "But he said I shouldn't go looking for Charlie and *Merrie*. There's no way he could have known my little girl's name unless—"

"The Jabberwock told him."

When Jolene pulled the van off the highway and into an overgrown "driveway," Stuart didn't at first recognize the Tibbits house because he and Cotton had come from the opposite direction.

Jolene turned off the ignition, but made no effort to get out. Neither did Stuart.

"Do you feel that?" she asked.

"I hoped it was just me."

Oppression. Irrational fear. What he'd felt in the driveway of Charlie's mother's house.

Jolene opened her door and got out, Stuart did the same on the other side and they both sucked in a gasp. It was *cold* here. That was nuts because they were standing outside on a summer day and it'd been nudging ninety degrees when they left Jolene's father's house. It'd been cloudy, but not *cold*.

Stuart watched his breath frost in front of him.

"Didn't think to pack my Nanook of the North coat," Jolene said, as she came around the van to open the side cargo door. "Silly me."

"Which one's the flux capacitor?"

"The what?"

"The machine Marty McFly used to go back to the future. Making jokes keeps me from screaming."

"Left my flux capacitor in my other suit."

Stuart turned toward the house.

"I'd forgotten what a dump this was." The roof over the front room of the house appeared to be stable, though the whole west end had collapsed, courtesy of a fallen tree that still lay there, toppled by some storm, or just died of old age. "Do we really have to go inside?"

"Yup. Inside is where the wild things are."

Stuart was hammered by longing so powerful it felt like a physical blow. *Where the Wild Things Are* was Merrie's favorite book.

There was no electricity here as there had been in Jolene's father's house — running water, too, all the comforts of home. But the equipment could run on battery power and the batteries were fully charged.

Stuart carefully stepped into the building, where the front door hung open on a lone rusty hinge. The front room was rectangular, with the door on the far end of the east side. On the left side of the front door, a big hole yawned in the side of the building where there had once been a picture window, though not so much as a piece of broken glass remained now. Three door-less doorways lead out of the front room, two on the north side directly across from the front door and another in the west side. That one was an archway that probably lead into the dining room. They set up the equipment on the east wall. With no doorway, it provided a long bare spot where they could place the wheeled cart — which Stuart had to wrestle into the building because there was no sidewalk to roll it along.

The place smelled like a dank, cold cellar. Musty. But more than musty. It smelled like … Stuart backed up from the thought, from the memory of the dream of dead bodies.

"Think there's a dead rat in here somewhere?" Jolene asked and he merely shrugged, not trusting himself to speak. "As cold as it is, maybe the thing's been frozen for a hundred years and just thawed out."

They quickly ferried in the equipment and placed it in position on the cart, both anxious to conduct their business and be gone. If Jolene had even hinted that she'd changed her mind, didn't want to perform the experiments after all, Stuart would cheerfully have turned tail and run. She didn't. Instead, she flipped switches, tinkered with settings, and the pleasant hum of the equipment coming to life helped mask what Stuart was steadfastly denying he could hear. Whispers. Voices.

"You ready?"

"As I'll ever be."

Jolene flipped three red switches in quick succession, then reached out and took his hand and pulled him with her away from the equipment into the middle of the room. She didn't let go of his hand.

"Showtime," she whispered.

HOWIE WITHERSPOON WOULD HAVE LOST his shirt at poker. His every emotion was stamped on his ugly face. But it wasn't just his face that telegraphed everything going on inside him. His whole body was a quivering mass of messaging, his body language shouting his guilt to the rooftops, fear sweat wafting up off him like stink off pole cat roadkill.

Malachi watched the little man squirm, disgusted by his sniveling subservience. He was more than a little drunk.

He had rushed up to Viola in that strange, hitching gait of his and Malachi could have sworn he almost fell to his knees in front of her. At the very least he wanted to reach out and kiss her ring.

Gratefully, he'd thought better of both those inappropriate responses and held fire just in time, merely began a whiney babble in a voice pitched too high for a man. Fear might have been squeezing his vocal cords, making it difficult to produce sound with them, but more likely the guy didn't manufacture enough testosterone to produce a sufficiently masculine sound. Safe money was on Door Number Two — a man who'd beat his wife wasn't really a man by anybody's definition.

"I got here as fast as I could, Mrs. Tackett, jumped in my car and drove as fast as I could. You said to come right away. Well, your boy said you wanted to see me right away and I'd have gotten here sooner if—"

Viola'd finally had enough.

"Shut up, Howie," she said.

Howie shut up.

A handful of people still milled around in the back of the courtroom and Viola directed Zach to shoo them out into the hallway, shut the door and not let anybody else inside, leaving only Malachi, Neb and Zach to watch the show.

Malachi leaned back against the railing that separated the room, crossed his arms over his chest and waited while his brother cleared the room. Then his mother turned and walked back up on the platform and sat down in the chair behind it. From this angle Malachi could see that the chair was rolled up to its highest position, leaving his mother's feet to dangle a couple of inches off the floor when she sat down.

But the little-kid-in-a-grownup-chair image didn't

translate from in front of the platform, where she could be seen leaning over the judge's "bench" and glaring at Howie Witherspoon, who'd been left standing alone before her.

The image put Malachi in mind of a frog in a cardboard box, looking up through the hole in the lid at the huge eye of a little kid. It wasn't out of the realm of possibility that Howie Witherspoon would wet his pants.

Viola'd just opened her mouth to speak when Obie peeked in the door through which the scraps of a crowd had just been moved out into the hallway.

"Whaddaya want us to do with him, Mama?" he asked.

Obie looked the most like their mother, though he was the most pleasant of the three, always had a smile on his face, in contrast to the scowl so deeply imprinted on Viola Tackett's features Malachi was certain it would remain there when she died. Obie wasn't smiling now, though. It was always hard for Malachi to watch his brothers struggle with the rudimentary mental tasks most people took for granted. Whenever any one of them was uncertain or confused, they turned to their mother for direction as unwaveringly as a four-year-old. And like small children, they were always uncertain the response they'd get for their intrusion into the affairs of grownups.

Obie'd been left to take down the body of Dylan Shaw, whose only crime was that he had stumbled into a useful position as a pawn in his mother's chess game. She had hung him with no more compassion than she'd have shown to a roach she stepped on scurrying across the kitchen floor. Now the kid was nothing more than meat, a body to dispose of.

Malachi tried to think like a soldier. As a soldier, you had to be able to let things like that go. Fallen comrades couldn't be mourned, not at the time anyway. Lose a step grieving over a friend and your buddies would be grieving over your body next. Every soldier mastered the mindset of setting aside emotion for another time and Malachi had been as good at that as most. But he couldn't summon that way of thinking now. Dylan Shaw wasn't a soldier who'd fallen in battle. He was a kid Malachi's mother had murdered, a young man whose dead body was now her only concern.

"Figure it out your own self," Viola snapped at Obie, knowing full well he was incapable, but knowing also that he'd find somebody standing around who'd help him come up with something. Folks would be very willing indeed now, to help out the Tacketts, to provide for them any service they needed.

"Yes ma'am," Obie said and closed the door.

Viola turned her attention to the smarmy little man standing below her. Which had been calculated, of course. She'd climbed back up there in the judge's seat for the express purpose of using her position there for intimidation. Malachi couldn't figure out why, though. She already intimidated the man, and this time when she handed down a guilty verdict, she would at least be serving justice.

"Now you, Howie. You gonna tell me what you done with your dead wife's body or are you gonna make me drag it out of you?"

Howie Witherspoon wet his pants.

Chapter Twenty-Nine

THAT JUDGE LADY had told Toby to stay in the room where the man put him, but she didn't say nothing about where in the room he was supposed to stay. So Toby crossed to the door leading back into the courtroom as soon as the man left, opened the door a crack, and tried to see and hear what was going on in the courtroom. He could hear fairly well. The judge woman was talking to a man who called her Mama. They were having an argument. It wasn't like Toby Witherspoon had never before heard grownups argue. He'd spent his life listening to it, except he didn't. When his parents started going at it, Toby did his dead level best not to hear it. Would get in his bed sometimes and put the pillow over his head. But even with the pillow over his head he could hear his mother screaming when his daddy hit her.

He tried to pay attention to this argument, but he didn't understand what it was about and it was always easy to figure out what his parents were fighting about.

His father had come home late. His father had been

drinking too much. His father was out "catting around," but Toby didn't know what that meant.

Or his mother had not ironed his father's shirt to suit him. Or she had let his dinner get cold when he came home late to eat it. Or she spent too much money or too much time on the telephone or was too fat or too loud or too …

These people weren't fighting about anything like that so Toby tuned them out. He wanted to sit down on the floor, was more tired than could be explained by riding his bike the four or five miles from his house into town. He was tired somewhere that wasn't about his arms and legs. Tired somewhere deep inside that was about who he was, worn out there from being afraid all the time. And missing his mother. She wasn't coming home; even if the Jabberwock lifted, she wasn't ever coming back. And thinking about that made him tired in the deep place where he wanted to go to sleep and not ever wake up.

Then he heard his father's voice and pulled the door open wider to listen and saw his father come running into the room. His father was hot and sweaty, like he was the one that'd ridden a bicycle into town instead of driving in an air-conditioned car. He looked worse than he'd looked last night. All the bruising was worse, the black eyes darker, the nose more swollen, the lip all puffed out. He had wrapped a huge bandage around his hand.

His father started talking, too fast, sounded like Toby'd sounded when he told the judge lady his story. He'd known he was talking too fast, needed to slow down so she could catch everything he was saying, but he hadn't been able to slow down and he figured his father wasn't able to slow down now. Then the judge lady told his father to shut up and he did.

Toby waited.

Then he heard the judge lady ask his father, flat out what he had done with his wife's body. Just flat out asked. She had believed Toby. She had. She didn't even need to go out to his house and dig up ...

What happened after that was confusing. Toby thought he knew what was going on, but then it didn't make any sense. The judge lady made his father admit what he'd done. It didn't take her long, and his father had cried when he talked about it, was trying to make the judge lady feel sorry for him, like what he'd done was an accident, that he hadn't meant to kill her. Surely the judge lady was too smart to fall for that excuse.

And she didn't seem to. She spoke to his father real mean, told him she'd ought to string him up from the pole out in front of the building like she'd just done that kid. The one Toby'd seen who'd wet his pants before he died.

The part Toby didn't understand came next. She talked about how she was in charge and everybody had to do things her way. About loyalty, not double crossing your partners. She talked about needing people she could count on, about how he'd owe her his life, about how she would draw and quarter him, use tractors instead of horses, whatever that meant, if he wasn't faithful and loyal.

None of that had anything to do with his father killing his mother. Then she'd told that man to "go get the boy," and he had time to close the door and go stand against the far wall before the man came in so he didn't know Toby'd been listening.

When Toby came out into the courtroom, he knew something really, really bad had happened. His father looked happy. The man who'd been arguing with the judge lady looked like he was so mad he was likely to explode. And the judge lady looked at Toby like he wasn't even there. The man led him out into the room and made him stand right beside his father. Toby smelled something, sniffed, then looked. He couldn't believe it, but the proof was right there, the dark stain. His father had *wet his pants*.

"You, son, I want you to listen up," the judge lady told him. "You ain't gonna go around spreading stories about your father no more, you hear me?"

Toby said nothing, didn't know he was supposed to answer until she said all mean-like, "I asked you a question, boy."

"I ... yes, I hear you. But ... what are you going to do about my daddy killing—" That's as far as he got before his father slapped him, knocked him off his feet so hard he hit the marble floor and slid across it.

"That's what I'm talking about," the judge lady said. "Them lies about your daddy killing your mother. You ain't gonna tell them lies no more, you hear me?"

Toby's cheek was on fire and his nose was bleeding. He could feel the trickle of blood beneath it. He felt the trickle run down his lip when he sat up and looked at the lady.

"Yes ma'am, I hear you." He wasn't afraid and he should have been. He should have been scared to death because it was plain that what'd happened was the judge lady had sided with his father and not with Toby. But Toby wasn't scared. He just felt tired. That tired from way down in the bottom of himself, the tired that made him just want to sleep.

"'Cause if you do open up your trap again," his father said, "you gonna wish you hadn't."

Toby looked up at his father. He'd seen that look in his father's eye before, right before he started beating on Toby's mother with his belt.

The judge lady gestured to the garbage bag on the floor that Toby'd used to carry his mother's purse on his bicycle. The purse was lying on the floor beside it.

"You ought to have burned it," she told his father and threw something at him which he tried to catch and missed. It tumbled to the floor. It was his mother's wallet.

Then she told his father to "take your snot-nosed brat and get out of here."

That's when the man who'd been leaning against the railing kind of exploded. He'd just been watching, looking mad, but he suddenly started shouting at the judge lady, telling her she couldn't be serious, that she wasn't really going to send a little boy home with his murderous father, that she couldn't—

And then she yelled back. Except she didn't yell. She just spoke in a normal voice but it was so mean-sounding it was like she was yelling. She told him that this wasn't none of his concern, and if he tried to make it his concern, "…your little friend Charlie's gonna get a visit from me."

The man shut up. It was like she'd slapped him the way Toby's father had slapped Toby.

Toby's father reached for the garbage bag and wallet on the floor, but the woman barked, "Leave it." So he grabbed Toby by the arm and glared at him. There was murder in his eyes.

That's what it was, a rage cranked up higher than any he'd displayed toward Toby's mother. It was probably the look he had in his eye, the last look she ever saw there. And then Toby *was* afraid. Not tired anymore, terrified. So scared he would have wet his own pants if he had needed to go.

His father yanked on his arm, and Toby looked at the man who had argued with his mother. Their eyes met and locked for a heartbeat, then his father yanked again and dragged Toby away.

Chapter Thirty

MALACHI TACKETT WOULD HAVE bet everything he owned, which, granted, wasn't a whole lot, that he was incapable of being surprised by anything his mother did.

He was dead wrong. As soon as he realized where his mother was going in her conversation with Howie Witherspoon, he was so shocked he really couldn't think of much at all.

She was going to let the slime bag go. She was willing to hang an innocent kid for something he didn't do, but unwilling to punish a murderer.

Blackmail, pure and simple. Oh, Viola Tackett didn't need anything to hold over a person's head to induce them to do her bidding and to convince them she would make them pay if they didn't. She would drop anybody at a whim and the whole county knew it. But for some reason, she'd decided to make this beat-up monster a slave on some higher order of magnitude. A slave squared. She'd made it clear to him that she wouldn't just kill him if he ever dared to let her down, she would draw and quarter him. Right there in the street in front of the courthouse.

She'd tie his arms and legs to tractors and literally rip him apart.

Why?

Why did she …?

And then Malachi let it go. There might not even be a reason why she'd done it, and if there was it was so sick and twisted Malachi would never be able to figure it out.

Even so, even after all that, Malachi didn't grasp that she meant to give the man back his kid until she did it. He assumed Viola would find somewhere to stick the boy, find some relative or neighbor. Make the boy shut up about his father, sure, scare him into keeping silence, but find him somewhere to go that was safe. Nope. She tossed the boy right back into the jaws of the lion that had eaten his mother.

Malachi went postal.

He stormed across the room toward his mother, shouting. He should have held onto his temper better than that, but as soon as he realized that she was actually going to … he lost it.

"Mama you can't do that!"

"There ain't nothing I can't do."

"You can't send that kid back home with the—"

"I can send that kid to the moon on a Frisbee if I want to."

"Don't you realize—?"

"Don't you realize this ain't none of your concern?"

"How can you possibly—?"

"I can because I can, and you need to back off and go mind your own business."

Before he could say another word, she spoke softly. "Or your little friend Charlie's gonna get a visit from me."

Malachi was shocked into silence. Found that not only could he not speak, he couldn't even breathe. His mother tossed the evidence of the man's crime back at him, told him to burn it, then told the guy to take his kid and get out.

The man grabbed the boy by the arm with his unbandaged hand and when he did the boy's terrified eyes found Malachi's. The terror in him was too great to be contained in the eyes of a little boy not yet tall enough to ride the rollercoaster at the fair.

The fear leapt across the room like a lightning bolt and slammed into Malachi's chest. This wasn't the first time he'd seen a look of fear like that on a little boy's face.

THE MURDERING HUTUS STAND ASIDE, bloody instruments of death in their hands, wild-eyed, crazed by drugs and blood lust, waiting for the Americans to leave before they fall on the hut full of Tutsi villagers and massacre them all.

Then a woman bursts out the door of the house and runs toward the American soldiers, she carries a baby and is dragging a boy of about eight by the arm.

"Take my children," she cries at the soldiers. "Save them."

The Hutu with a scar on his face takes two great strides and slashes into her back with a machete and she drops the baby. Another one with a sharpened stick impales the infant with it. But the little boy makes it to the soldiers, to Malachi, grabs hold of him in a death grip and tries to hide behind him.

Malachi glances down into the boy's face. The terror in his eyes bores all the way through layers of military training and professional detachment into the core of the human being who is Malachi Tackett.

MALACHI HAD SHOT the Hutu with a machete advancing on the boy. Had swung his rifle around ready to mow down every one of the other monsters. But his best friend had knocked him unconscious, saved him from the consequences of an act that would likely have set off an international incident.

When Malachi'd come to and asked about the boy, his friend had told him the murdering Hutus had cut off his head, gave it to Malachi's sergeant as a present for Malachi.

Malachi stepped obediently back to the railing and watched the father drag his son out of the courtroom. Waited for his mother to finish giving directions to his brothers.

"You ain't got no truck. How'd you get here?" his mother asked him, then answered her own question before he had a chance. "Rode with that McClintock woman, did you?" She smiled. "I seen she had the good judgment to make herself scarce. You can ride with me, but we ain't going out Gizzard Ridge. I got new digs."

"New digs? You were born in that house."

"Ain't gonna die in it, though!"

When she told him what she'd done, the only words he could force out between his lips were, "Where's Sebastian?"

"He's out there somewhere." Her voice was dismissive. "Hope he's 'roughing it' in some place don't have no indoor plumbing."

As they walked out of the room together, she went on and on about the Nower house she had stolen, how pretty it was inside, how Essie had her own room that had a lacy bedspread and a feather mattress.

"Why, they's even little candles sitting in little bitty vases on the back of the toilet."

"They're called votive candles, Mama."

"Huh?"

"Never mind."

"They smell real good when you light them — cinnamon and vanilla and the like — but ain't no stink for them to cover up 'cause when you hit flush it all goes away."

She laughed at that. Saw that he didn't.

"Ain't no sense in getting yore nose all outta joint 'bout things you ain't got no control over." She stopped. He continued on a couple of steps then turned back to her. "And you ain't got no control over none of this — we clear on that, ain't we?" She cocked her head to the side and plastered a phony look of sympathy on her face. "'Cause it sure would be a pure-D shame if they was a little half-breed girl suddenly become an orphan, 'thout no mama to look after her. Kids like her don't usually fare too well among decent folk."

He managed to keep his hands from balling into fists, but couldn't keep the contempt off his face.

"Bigotry doesn't become you, Mama. Makes the hard lines around your mouth deeper … and you could just about eat pudding out of them now."

She didn't even get angry, just shook her head. "You keep fooling around, son, and you gonna make me mad. You really don't want to make me mad."

"You're right. I don't want to make you mad. A woman who could do what you did here today in cold blood … God only knows what you'd be capable of if you got riled up."

He saw her jaw tighten, her eyes narrow, and he backed off, took a breath, kept his voice level.

"Look … I can't do this." He made a vague gesture that took in everything and nothing. "I need some space, some air. I need to walk—"

"It's that PTSD thing, ain't it?"

Malachi was stunned. He had no idea his mother knew

anything about post-traumatic stress disorder. She saw his surprise.

"You ain't been around enough as a grown man, leaving like you done. You think you know me, but you don't. You ain't got no idea what all I know."

Malachi drew on reserves of strength he didn't know he had to force the next words out his mouth.

"Do you … still know how to make pole beans with ham hock, and cornbread? It's been years since …"

She actually smiled. It even looked genuine.

"Why shore I do! Sebastian Nower had his own little garden right beside the back porch. I could even whip up a mess of fried okra or turnip greens."

When they got out to the front of the building the crowd had cleared away. There was nothing left on the steps to indicate that a teenager had been murdered there only a short time ago.

Malachi couldn't make himself smile, couldn't if he'd had a gun to his head. But he did nod, turned to walk away.

"Where you goin'?" She was suspicious.

"Obviously nowhere I can't walk to." That seemed to mollify her. "I'm not staying in the Nower House, Mama. Neb can take me back to the Middle of Nowhere after supper. We're taking turns looking after E.J. — Sam, Charlie, Judd Perkins, Raylynn and—"

"You hadn't ought to be wearing yourself out—"

He held up his hand and stopped her cold.

"Not your circus. Not your monkey."

Then he turned and ambled off down Mail Street in the opposite direction from the Nower House.

"I'll keep it hot for you," she called after him. "Ain't no hurry. Whenever you're ready."

He didn't trust himself to turn back around, just kept walking.

Malachi had no vehicle. He could call Charlie or Sam to come give him a ride, but he had no intention of dragging the two of them into what he was planning to do. There were other people he could ask, of course, but once his mother found out what Malachi'd done — and he wouldn't be able to hide the deed forever — she'd come down with both feet on everybody involved. He couldn't ask anybody to chance running afoul of his mother's temper.

Then he thought about the boy. How had Toby Witherspoon gotten here? If they hadn't moved, and nobody in Nowhere County *moved*, the Witherspoons lived on Iron Rock Road, the second or third house down from the Wiley Road turnoff. The kid surely hadn't hitched a ride, not carrying a sack that contained his murdered mother's purse. And that was quite a hike for an eight-year-old. Then Malachi and his mother'd stepped out onto the porch of the courthouse and he'd spotted a bicycle leaned against the big flower pot out front.

It wasn't exactly the means of transportation Malachi would have picked — a Humvee would have been more to his liking — but he was in no position to be choosy. Gratefully, it was a big 10-speed. He had learned in the Marine Corps that the best battle plan in the world only lasted until the first shot was fired. Everything after that was improvisation. He was improvising and the bicycle was a peg up from walking. But he'd have *crawled* out to the Witherspoon place if he'd had to, to save that kid. And from the look on the boy's father's face, Malachi couldn't get there soon enough.

Chapter Thirty-One

TOBY SCRUNCHED himself up tight against the passenger door as his father drove out of the Ridge down Wiley Road headed home. He wanted to get as far away from his father as he could because he was afraid. And because his father stank. He had wet himself.

But he must have still been a little drunk because he didn't seem to notice. The man was in a grand mood.

"Planning on jumping out of the car, are you? I wouldn't recommend it. You'd get the mother of all skinned knees on the asphalt." His tone turned cold. "And I'd pick you up off the road and throw you in the backseat, or maybe the trunk, and take you home anyway."

Toby said nothing. What was there to say?

"Why'd you do it?"

Toby didn't answer. His father let go of the wheel with his right hand for a moment, drew back to hit him and Toby put up his hands to protect his face.

"You said Mama went shopping with her sister on Jabberwock Day, but she didn't. I saw her that day."

"Oh no, son, you're mistaken." He ground out the next

words through clenched teeth. "Remember what Judge Tackett said. You got to quit making up them lies about me." He paused. "I been ordered by the judge to beat it out of you if you ever say anything like that about me again. You got that?"

Toby nodded, saw the look on his father's face and said, "Yes … sir."

"Where'd you get your mama's purse?"

"Custard brought it to me. She dug it up … somewhere."

"Soon's I get home, I'm gonna kill that dog.

"No, please don't. She didn't mean—"

He did hit Toby then. A backhanded blow aimed at his face but Toby was able to scrunch away so it caught him in the shoulder.

"Don't you tell me what I can and can't do. Your mama tried that, and it didn't work out too well for her."

"You killed her, didn't you?"

Toby couldn't believe he'd said it, but for some deep and compelling reason he had to hear his father tell him to his face what he'd done. He hadn't meant to blurt it out like that, though, and was so horrified his father must have seen the shocked look on his face because he threw his head back and laughed, a full, hearty belly laugh.

"Yeah, I killed her. But I wasn't lying when I told Viola Tackett it was an accident. It was. I didn't intend to kill her. She accused me of screwing around on her, said she knew it was Hayley and she was gonna tell the pig's father … so I hit her. Lost my temper and kept hitting her until …"

He paused.

"There, you happy now? I admitted it. I killed your mother. Accidental." He paused, reached up to touch his swollen lip and a look of raw fury washed over his face. "Wasn't no accident the second time. I meant to kill *her.*

Planned it and—" He stopped, looked at Toby and the rage was gone from his face. It had been replaced by a look that was cold and calculating, a look with murderous intent behind it, churning around ideas, planning.

That look told Toby that his father intended to kill him. Maybe not today or tomorrow. But he would eventually. He had to. He couldn't allow the boy to grow up into a man who knew his father had killed his mother. Toby figured it'd likely be sooner rather than later, while his father was still in the good graces of the judge lady. Toby didn't figure she would be the least upset to find out that Howie's little boy had got lost in the woods and his father couldn't find him.

When his father pulled up into the driveway, Toby leapt out of the car and ran into the house, where Custard was standing in front of the door yapping furiously. He snatched her up into his arms and kept running. Out the back door and into the woods. He didn't even realize he was sobbing until he almost ran into a tree because his vision was so blurred by tears. But he didn't stop, even when Custard began to wiggle and squirm because he was holding her so tight. He just kept running. And crying.

~

NOTHING HAPPENED.

Stuart and Jolene stood in the middle of the cold living room of Reece Tibbits' falling-down shack, waiting for something awful.

Nothing.

When they had encountered the beasties at Jolene's father's house, the response had been immediate. She didn't even have to turn it all on before company showed up and the freakshow started. A bleeding ceiling, screaming white faces.

Stuart figured his voice would be shaky, but he spoke anyway.

"Don't guess now is the time to ask if it's plugged in, huh?

Jolene let go of his hand and walked to the equipment on the equipment cart beside the front door. She fiddled with gauges, switched switches. She even thumped one of the dials with her finger, but it wasn't stuck.

"I might as well be in one of my not-real haunted houses," she said with her back still to him. "But I set all the dials back to zero, all the default settings, so I couldn't even fake a presence here."

"If there's nothing here, why is it so cold?" Stuart asked.

She turned back toward him. "That, I couldn't tell—"

She stopped in mid-sentence and she wasn't looking at Stuart. She was looking at the front window behind him, the broke-out picture window on the front of the house.

The hair on the back of Stuart's neck stood on end, and he should have been so frightened he'd turn immediately around, maybe leap away. But he was so scared he couldn't move at all for a few seconds. And some part of him didn't want to know what was behind him.

"... like you described ... what you saw on the road ..."

Jolene was having trouble forming words.

Then reaction caught up with him and he spun around, arms up to ward off a blow. What he saw knocked the air out of him as surely as any tackle ever had.

The hole where the window had been was gone. In its place was a ... blank space. There was no other way to describe it. It was like there had been the remains of a window there before and you could see through it to Jolene's van parked out front and then someone erased the part inside the window frame.

But it wasn't completely blank and Stuart instantly saw what Jolene was talking about. In the center of the blankness was a hole, small, the size of a golf ball.

The hole didn't stay small. No sirree, it sure didn't. It expanded. Like the aperture on a camera, making the hole wider and wider. Just like what had happened on the highway yesterday as dust from an explosion settled out of the sky. Only in reverse. Instead of a shrinking reality, this was an expanding reality.

Now it was the size of a baseball.

Now a basketball.

Irrational thoughts fired through his sparking synapses.

It wouldn't ever be the size of a football because footballs weren't round, a fact Merrie had pointed out to him the first time she tried to bounce one on the floor.

Ball analogies finally became useless because the hole was the size of a washing machine, then a Volkswagen, and growing steadily bigger.

Stuart saw Jolene look from him to the front door and back. Maybe if she made a break for the door … but she didn't. She was suddenly beside him, grabbing his hand. They backed away from the opening hole together until they felt the wall against their backs and they couldn't back up anymore. By then both of them could see that the hole was not opening up to reveal what was on the other side of the window, the van parked outside. The hole was opening up to reveal a man.

Reece Tibbits.

Chapter Thirty-Two

TOBY FINALLY COLLAPSED, fell to his knees in front of a huge oleander bush that covered the whole base of a big oak tree. He parted the dangling branches and crawled into the dark, buggy interior until he was completely out of sight. Then he gave in to his tears for a time, he didn't know how long.

How did you think about your father wanting to kill you? Where was a place for that in your head? Surely, he was wrong, just misjudged his father's intent. Surely, he could just take Custard and go back home and his father would be sitting in his chair getting quietly drunk, and he'd tell Toby to make himself a sandwich and then Toby would go take a bath and go to bed and everything would be all right.

How very, very desperately Toby wanted to believe that. He didn't believe it, but he *wanted to* almost bad enough to go home. There was a part of him that hurt so bad he didn't really want to escape from his father.

Oh, sure, he had believed his father had killed his mother, had been convinced of it before he ever found her purse. He thought he'd heard his father confess to the judge lady. But maybe he'd misunderstood. It was hard to hear through that crack. He could have been wrong. Until his father confessed to *him*, the tiny flame of hope that Toby wouldn't even admit he clung to still flickered. That his mother really was alive somewhere, that she just couldn't get back home, like all the other people who'd been locked out by the Jabberwock. But one day the Jabberwock would be gone and his mother would come back and throw her arms around him and he would hug her tight and smell her—

No. That was never going to happen.

His mother was dead, buried in the compost heap.

His father had killed her, just like he would kill Toby if he caught him. No, that was crazy. He wouldn't do a thing like that, kill his own son. Fathers didn't kill their own children.

They didn't, did they?

Toby couldn't know a thing like that for sure. So wasn't it better, really, just to give up, let whatever was going to happen happen? Did he really want to live in the world knowing for absolute certain that he'd never see his mother again? Knowing for absolute curtain that his father had killed her? Wouldn't it be better—?

And some big thing in Toby exploded in his chest.

No!

He would not just roll over and let his father kill him. If he did, his father'd get away with it and with killing Toby's mother … and with the other murder, the one his father said he'd "planned."

I meant to kill her!

His father had reached up and touched his swollen lip when he said that. He had killed whoever it was who'd beaten him up, had done it on purpose.

Hayley.

Toby's mother had found out about *Hayley* and was going to tell "the pig's" father. Hayley *Norman* — the fat girl who had been Toby's Vacation Bible School teacher. Her father was the minister of the church … and Toby's father had *killed* her.

Two. His father had committed murder — *twice*.

He'd do it again, too.

No pretending anymore.

No more doubts.

If Toby's father caught him, he'd—

Custard had been sitting quietly in Toby's lap. She'd given up trying to squirm out of his grip. But now she suddenly started barking furiously, that awful yap-yap-yapping sound.

Somebody was coming.

IT HAD to be Reece Tibbits. Jolene didn't remember the man from when she was growing up, but the description Stuart had given fit him perfectly. Big and broad-shouldered, wearing bib overalls with a tee shirt beneath, and his hair. The white streak, the lightning bolt, it was there.

Of course, she wasn't looking at his hair. As soon as Jolene could see his face, she could look at nothing else. Her grandmother's words returned to her. The old woman had caught her crossing her eyes in front of mirror. "You make faces like that, your face is gonna freeze. Then what will you do?"

Reece Tibbits's face had frozen. His features weren't mobile. They were as solid in place as a sculpture. And maybe this was a sculpture. A mannequin and not a man. Maybe it was a statue.

Yes ... maybe a statue, because the skin color wasn't right. Pale, too pale.

The look that froze his face was the single most horrified visage Jolene had ever seen. His eyes were transfixed on some great horror beyond human comprehension, and the rest of his face was drawn up in a rictus of terror.

She had to look away, and when she did, she saw that Reece Tibbits was not alone.

He must have brought his whole family home with him.

A woman and two teenage girls stood to his left and slightly behind him. The woman — his wife? — was skinny, wearing worn jeans and a faded University of Kentucky tee shirt, her hair caught back in a limp brown ponytail.

The oldest of the two girls was in full-bore adolescence, sporting a bumper crop of pimples all over her face, the kind that made you cringe because you wanted somebody to pop them.

The younger girl had pretty blonde hair. It curled around her face — which was the wrong color somehow. It didn't look like ... real skin. It was sallow and so very, very pale. Her lips were blue. All their lips were blue. She was the image of her father.

Of course they all looked like Reece now because all their faces were frozen in identical, though individual, looks of abject terror.

It was like a family portrait snapped when they'd all looked up to see a charging elephant bearing down on them.

"They're ... holograms," she whispered, her voice airless. "They are, aren't they?"

She thought he nodded, but maybe he shook his head.

She couldn't tell because she was unable to drag her eyes off the tableau to look at Stuart's face.

"The aperture" thing was fully open now, floor to ceiling, from one edge of the window to the other. They'd been staring straight ahead, sightlessly — no, like they were looking at something awful in front of them that you couldn't see. Then they all looked at Jolene and somebody started screaming, wailing a high horrified cry that sounded like the sail on a ship ripping from top to bottom. It was several seconds before Jolene realized she was the one screaming, so transfixed in horror was she at the four figures that stood only a few feet away.

Their faces remained frozen, but they had all cut their eyes toward her *in unison* — without moving their heads. Snap, four sets of eyes staring at her out of horrified, terrified faces. But the look in the eyes wasn't fear. The faces were afraid. The eyes were angry. Furious, raging. The bodies before them might be Reece Tibbits and his wife and daughters. But whatever was behind the eyes — it was the Jabberwock.

Chapter Thirty-Three

Toby tried to shut Custard up, but there was no silencing her. The fur on the back of her neck was standing up and she was in full-bore yap mode, and when she got that way she wouldn't shut up until she felt like it.

"Go away," he whispered to her fiercely. "Go back to the house."

But she wouldn't budge, stood her ground between him and the concealing branches of the bush.

Then a voice spoke from beyond the branches, and when Toby peered out through them he could see the shoes of somebody standing next to the oak tree.

"Come on out, boy," his father said. "You think I don't know you're hiding in there with the dog?"

Toby considered refusing. Thought about making his father drag him out, kicking and screaming. But that awful tiredness washed over him again, taking all his strength. He wanted to resist, but he was just too tired.

The dog kept yapping. When Toby parted the branches of the oleander bush and crawled out, she went with him, hopping around his father's feet in a yapping frenzy. Toby was surprised the dog wasn't quick enough to dodge the blow, but his father's foot shot out too fast. The toe of his shoe connected with the side of the dog, lifted her off the ground like one of those guys on the football field, kicking a ball off that little tee thing they set up in the ground.

Custard emitted only a single pain-filled yip, then her body flew through the air and connected with a tree trunk, making a sickening thud sound. She lay there at the base of the tree. Still. Blood leaked out the corner of her mouth.

"Shoulda killed that dog a long time ago," his father said. "Useless mutt. Wasn't worth the bullet it'd a took to put her down."

That's when Toby noticed the knife in his father's hand. His father saw him notice it and an unreadable look crossed his face, was gone almost as quickly as it came. Pity, maybe. Sympathy. It had been a kind emotion of some sort but it could find no purchase in the folds of his father's hard face.

"I don't want to hurt you, son."

Toby began to back away.

"This can go easy, or hard. I didn't never want you to be a party to this. But you couldn't keep your nose out of it. Taking your mama's purse to Viola Tackett like you done. Didn't leave me no choice."

Shifting the blame. A little observation flitted through Toby's mind then and was gone. Nothing was ever his father's fault. His mother should have had supper ready on time. She shouldn't have nagged him. Toby should have kept his nose out of his father's business. Everything would be fine in his father's life if the people around him would just do what *they* were supposed to do. And when they didn't ... well, it certainly wasn't Howie Witherspoon's fault when they got what was coming to them.

Toby shook his head as he backed away, a knot of fear in his throat so he could barely speak.

"Please ..." That was all he could get out. The one word. It sounded so tiny and weak and pitiful. Toby didn't want to sound like that, wanted to sound strong and brave.

But he was eight years old and neither strong nor brave.

And his father was about to kill him.

JOLENE WAS STANDING BESIDE STUART, shrieking, the sound assaulting his ears.

Then Reece Tibbits opened his mouth.

Before he could speak, a bug crawled across his tongue and fell off the end of it to the floor.

The shrieking turned up in volume and in shrillness, a sound so sharp it sliced into his ears, seemed to shred his eardrums.

"I warned you," said a voice that came out of the throat of Reece Tibbits. It was a hoary sound, like chains dragged slowly across a metal floor. The words themselves carried no threat, were as lifeless as the frozen faces. But there was anger in the eyes. Raging fury. "You can't have them. They're *mine*."

Stuart could see now that there were things crawling on all of them, bugs, creatures with many legs and shiny bodies. Beetles. Scarabs.

It's not real! His mind screamed the words inside the confines of his skull and they bounced around in there. They're holograms! Yeah, more lifelike than the others, but holograms.

Then the thing that was/wasn't Reece Tibbits moved, a lumbering, ungraceful motion with his hands out in front of him, fingers clenching and unclenching.

The woman and girls moved, too. Started for Jolene. The expressions on the faces never changed, though, remained frozen in terror. Only the eyes were alive, pulsing with blinding fury.

Stuart hadn't felt this sensation in years, but he slipped into the unreality of it as naturally as he had done so many, many times before. Time slowed down. The world on its axis stopped its normal spinning. Every sound, every movement, every sensation was stretched out, took too long to hear, to see and to feel.

Life in slow motion.

He had been gripped by the sensation every time he played a football game. He'd tried to ask other players if they felt something similar, but the looks on their faces told him they thought he wasn't dragging a full string of fish.

THE SNAP.

He turns to run his route.

Gets one step on the tackle.

Dodges a lineman.

Runs — his feet hitting the ground in individual impacts that shake his body, and he feels each vibration.

His head slowly revolves, turns to look back over his shoulder.

The ball is in the air, spiraling across the blue sky.

He reaches up.

Catches it.

Clutches it to his chest.

Feels the tackle on his heels grab him and the impact of hitting the ground, a grunt forced out of his chest.

. . .

STUART GRUNTED LIKE THAT NOW, a low, guttural sound he'd only ever made when he'd been slammed into the turf beneath a 250-pound tackle. Only now, he had been hammered with an emotional wallop that packed as much force and impact. The sight of the *creature* that was/wasn't Reece Tibbits lunging at him knocked all the wind out of Stuart.

Reece crossed the room in two long, clumsy strides and threw himself the rest of the way.

And the familiar slow-motion sensation carried Stuart along.

In a single graceful movement, Stuart crouched, lowered his right shoulder, and when the Tibbits thing was in position, just the right spot, Stuart exploded out of the crouch, driving his shoulder into the creature's midsection, bowling him over backwards.

Reece's clumsy collapse took his wife and one of the other girls down with him.

But the other girl, the older one with a pimpled face, had flung herself at Jolene, slammed her into the wall and then the two of them tumbled to the floor with the girl on top, her hands around Jolene's throat.

Chapter Thirty-Four

MALACHI WHEELED the bicycle into the Witherspoons' driveway and leapt off it, panting. The ride from town had been a workout and he was drenched in sweat and gasping for breath. Pulling his pistol out of his waistband, he approached the house from the driveway, careful to stay behind Witherspoon's car out of the line of sight from the windows on the front of the house.

He hadn't really formulated a plan, what he would do when he found Toby and his father. Though it was clear Howie Witherspoon had killed Toby's mother, Malachi wouldn't set himself up as judge and jury — and executioner. All he wanted was the boy, to take him away from his murderous father and keep him safe. Beyond that—

He suddenly heard the furious yapping of a small dog. It was coming from the woods behind the house. It must be the dog that had dug up Toby's mother's purse out of the compost heap. The yapping cut off suddenly, ended in a single pain-filled yip and then the woods were silent. Malachi took off running into the trees toward where the sound had been.

Malachi could see Howie and Toby through the trees ahead. Toby was backing away from his father, shaking his head. His father had a knife.

Then Howie reached out with the speed of a rattlesnake and grabbed Toby by the upper arm, yanked him almost off his feet as he lifted the knife above him.

"Drop the knife, Howie," Malachi called out.

THE FINGERS that encircled Jolene's throat were cold.

She registered the sensation, the unnaturalness of it.

Even as the force of the assault drove her against the wall, she felt the delicacy of the fingers, frail and skinny, like a baby bird's wings.

But squeezing. Squeezing tight.

Jolene couldn't breathe. No air in or out. Black spots appeared before her eyes as she fell sideways onto the floor, felt the blow when her head hit the boards, watched the world spin crazily, and a *whahm, whahm, whahm* sound reverberated in her ears.

The girl on top of her was no weight at all. A child. But the force of her fingers digging into the skin of Jolene's neck was stealing reality out of the world, graying out the edges of her vision.

And somewhere inside Jolene a little spark of anger ignited.

Nooooo!

It burst instantly into her own flame of rage.

I don't think so, sweetheart!

Jolene grabbed the wrists attached to the hands that choked her, squeezed as hard as she could and then yanked them apart. In the same motion, she lurched upward.

The girl let go, couldn't hold on, and fell away when Jolene rolled over on her side and dumped her off.

Before Jolene had time to do more than grab a single lungful of air, she felt a big hand encircle her wrist, nothing fragile and frail, a hold she could not possibly break.

She was literally yanked off the floor to her feet.

Stuart!

"Come on!" he yelled, dragging her along behind him as he made for the door. The instant they stepped out of the building, a blast of air so cold it would have frozen water droplets in the air pushed them forward. There was a sound behind them, a moaning sound, accompanied by whispers. Whispers fed into a microphone and their volume amplified until the sound was ear-splitting.

She didn't remember running to the van, just felt Stuart shove her in the side panel door they'd left open and slam it behind her. Then she heard the front door slam, the engine start, and lurched forward as the vehicle fishtailed in the dirt and shot forward down the road.

Somewhere along in there, Jolene Rutherford started to cry.

HOWIE WITHERSPOON almost jumped out of his skin when he heard the voice. He looked around frantically, trying to locate the source, but either didn't see very well or was too scared to focus because his eyes passed over Malachi and kept searching.

That gave Malachi another couple of seconds to cross more ground. He needed to get closer.

"Who are — *Malachi Tackett* — what are you doing—?" He yanked the boy to him, clutched him up tight against his chest with the hand that had an injured thumb, and held the knife to the boy's throat with his other hand. "You get on outta here and mind your own business. Your mama—"

"You let me worry about Mama. She's my problem. Now put the knife down."

His eyes snapped to where Malachi was advancing through the trees. He held the pistol out in front of him in a two-hand grip, which soldiers called "cop mode." Most military firearms training wasn't designed to prepare a soldier to stand out in the open with his weapon drawn, facing down a lone enemy.

"This ain't none of your concern—"

Malachi continued to advance and Howie appeared to realize he'd allowed him to get too close.

"Stop right there. I mean it. Stop or I will slit this kid's throat."

Malachi stopped.

"This doesn't have to end badly. Nobody has gotten hurt here, no harm, no foul. Let the boy go and I will—"

"Shoot me where I stand. You think I'm stupid? You think I don't know you're all 'Superman to the rescue' here, Army Ranger or Special Forces or whatever it is? I know your kind, think you're better than everybody else, think you're the meanest dog in the junkyard." The man straightened and actually puffed out his chest. "Well, you ain't. Not this time, you ain't. You done met your match, *hero*. Now, you turn around right now or this kid'll be dead before he hits the ground."

"And *then* I'll shoot you where you stand."

"Yeah, but the kid you done knocked yourself out to rescue'll be dead as roadkill. You ain't gonna let me do that."

He was right, Malachi was not going to let him do that. He still wasn't as close as he'd like. He could certainly land a lethal body shot or a simple headshot from this range, but he had to hit the T-zone for an instant kill. The T-zone was an area about an inch wide that stretched across the eyebrow ridge and the bridge of the nose. Though a shot anywhere in the head would be fatal, only a shot to the T-zone would sever the medulla, the lower base of the brain-stem, preventing brain signals from reaching the rest of the body. Instant death, not so much as the twitch of the fingers he had wrapped around the hilt of that knife.

"I'll give you to the count of three. One …"

Malachi had stopped with his feet spread wide for stability. Now, he steadied his hands, drew in a breath.

"Two … I mean it, Malachi. I'll do it! Thr—"

Malachi squeezed the trigger. A red blotch appeared on Howie Witherspoon's forehead at the bridge of his mangled nose. The knife dropped from his lifeless fingers and Howie Witherspoon was dead before he hit the ground.

Toby stood there as if his father still had a grip on his arm. His eyes were wide with terror and shock, but looking at the boy's face, Malachi felt a jubilant sense of triumph. He hadn't been able to save the other little boy, the one who'd clutched at his leg in terror in the nightmare world of Rwanda. But he had saved *this boy*.

Chapter Thirty-Five

SAM LEAPT out of the chair and rushed to the front window when they heard the car pull into her driveway, exchanging a terrified look with Charlie.

"Is it …?" Charlie didn't seem to have enough air to finish.

If Viola had come for her …

As soon as she and Sam had stopped shaking, sitting in Charlie's car in the parking lot, watching the crowd around the courthouse begin to disperse, they had agreed that hiding was futile. There wasn't a rock anywhere in the county Charlie could crawl under that Viola Tackett couldn't find her.

Either Malachi had talked his mother off the ledge or he hadn't. That was Charlie's only hope.

"It's Malachi," Sam said. She waited at the door, then opened it, but it wasn't Malachi who stepped inside. It was a little boy, the boy who'd climbed a tree to watch the hanging.

"This is Toby Witherspoon," Malachi said. Then to the boy, "Toby, this is Charlie McClintock and—"

"I know Miss Sheridan," the boy said in a small voice. "You came to the house after my mother broke …" He stopped, then started again with a tangle of emotions gripping his words. "When my father broke my mother's arm!"

Sam shot a look at Malachi.

"Toby's father killed his mother and tried to kill Toby."

"But Malachi shot him."

That was a conversation stopper.

Sam recovered first.

"Uh … how about you two have a seat," she said, and Charlie thought she sounded like Vanna White turning letters on the set of *Wheel of Fortune*.

Gratefully, Merrie — who'd been sitting on the floor playing with a magnifying glass from Rusty's chemistry set — rescued them all from awkward. She stood up with her feet spread far apart and announced to the group.

"I think I just pooped my pants."

After the kids were finally out from under foot, and after the huge pot of spaghetti Sam whipped up out of nowhere, Sam, Charlie and Malachi sat in Sam's living room sipping cups of really good coffee.

Charlie'd always admired women who could do a thing like that — walk into an empty kitchen, turn around three times and put a full meal on the table without so much as a dusting of flour on a countertop. Oh, Charlie could whip up a meal that fast. Easy peasy. It was called "carry-out" or "home delivery" or simply, "pizza."

Merrie was curled up asleep in the wingback chair, had conked out like somebody'd taken out her batteries. Rusty wasn't asleep, but he was upstairs in his room reading. His bedroom had bunkbeds. Charlie didn't know why, since Rusty was Sam's only child, but they'd installed an exhausted Toby in the bottom bunk with a comic book and told him he didn't have to go to sleep, could stay up as long as he wanted — knowing he'd pass out in five minutes.

A brief explanation and a few veiled references had painted a pretty accurate picture of what'd happened at Howie Witherspoon's house, but Malachi connected the rest of the dots.

"I sent Toby away, told him to wait in his father's car while I disposed of his father's body. I thought about burying it in the compost heap behind the garage." He paused. "Toby was right. That's where his father buried his mother, but Howie was too lazy to dig the grave deep enough to … it's bad back there. So I wrapped Howie's body in a tarp and put it in the garage and I'll figure out something to do with it tomorrow. And with the dog."

"The dog?" Sam asked.

"Howie killed Custard, his wife's dog. I promised Toby I'd bury the body."

"Now what?" Sam asked.

"Now, I need to take Howie's car back to his house." He looked at Sam. "And I need you to drop me off on Main Street in the Ridge so I can walk to the Nower House."

"Why there?"

"My mother stole it from Nower. She's living there now."

"Just like that," Sam said. It wasn't a question.

"Just like that. I told her I would come by for supper. I'll get one of my brothers to run me back out to the Middle of Nowhere, send Raylynn home a little early. Judd'll be there by four." A hint of a smile darted out to capture his face. "Once a dairy farmer, always a dairy farmer."

"And then …?" Sam asked.

Malachi turned apologetically to Charlie.

"I'm so sorry, Charlie. Now, you're right back in the frying pan. I'd bought you out until Toby came along. And I couldn't—"

She held up her hand. "Of course you couldn't."

Sam's phone rang and they all exchanged an apprehensive look.

How could the simple ringing of a telephone sound so ominous? Of course, it wasn't the sound. It was the context. The craziness, the understanding that nobody was getting calls anymore from people trying to sell them magazine subscriptions or an extended warranty on the family Buick. In the new normal of life in Nowhere County, no telephone call was likely to be innocuous.

"I'll get it, Mom," Rusty called from upstairs and the ringing stopped.

"There is only one way any of this ends well," Malachi said. "We have to get out of here, out of this county, back to the world where there are cops and jails … and execution chambers."

"And rabies vaccines."

Rusty came to the head of the stairs and told his mother, "I thought it'd be Douglas, but it's Mrs. Jackson. She wants to talk to you."

Sam went into the kitchen and picked up the downstairs extension, leaving Malachi and Charlie waiting in the living room. Malachi leaned back in the chair and closed his eyes. Charlie picked up her cup from the saucer on the coffee table and glanced at the bowl of seashells on the table beside it. The phone conversation was brief, then Sam returned.

"Thelma Jackson really wanted to talk to you," Sam told Charlie, and sat down beside her on the sofa. "She called your mother's number and when you didn't answer, she called me. She wants to talk about what you said at the meeting — the part about all of us putting our heads together to figure this thing out."

"At least one person was listening," Charlie said.

"I told her to come by the clinic in the morning." She looked for and got approval from Charlie and Malachi.

"Is there something specific she wants to tell us?" Charlie asked. She set her cup down and picked up a seashell out of the bowl, turned it over absentmindedly as she spoke.

"She didn't say ... did you know that besides teaching history, Thelma was a genealogy buff?"

She and Malachi shook their heads.

"Apparently, she's spent years tracing the ancestry of Nowhere people. She said we might be interested in what she found out about Gideon."

They all stiffened at the word.

"She said there'd been a village of settlers in that same spot by the waterfall in Fearsome Hollow back in the late 1700s."

"Seriously?" Charlie dropped the shell back into the bowl and picked up another one.

"Other people vanished there, *too?*" Malachi asked. "Before Gideon?"

Sam shrugged. "I guess we'll find out tomorrow." Charlie watched her try to connect the dots. "Gideon vanished in 1895 — a hundred years ago." She stopped. "In fact, I hadn't thought about it, but it was early summer ... it could have been a hundred years ago *to the day*." She rolled with it. "And if this other village was there in the *late 1700s* ... that could have been 1795. A hundred years before that." Sam's face lit up. "You don't suppose that every hundred years—"

"No, I don't," Malachi said. His voice was flat.

"But maybe—"

"Maybe what happened to Gideon and this other village are connected in some way," he said. "I don't know about that. But I don't think what's happening *right now* is about some every-hundred-years timing."

"If it's not happening now because it's a hundred years since the last time it happened — why *is* it happening now?" Sam asked.

No one answered. Charlie reached out to return the shell to the bowl and that's when she saw it. She picked it up and turned it over in her hand, then spoke softly.

"In fiction, the story starts with an 'inciting' incident. Something happens that changes the normal status quo."

Sam continued the thought. "So Nowhere County was chugging along, all of us Nowhere people doing our nowhere things and then suddenly, *bam!* — the Jabber-wock. What changed?"

Charlie held out the piece of a geode in the palm of her hand.

"This is the rock the witch gave you, isn't it?" she asked Sam.

Sam smiled. "Yeah, it's been in the shell bowl all these years."

"The witch gave us the rocks for a reason, so we wouldn't forget her warning not to come back," Charlie said. "Remember? She said we shouldn't have gone into the woods, that we had made it *want*."

"No, it wasn't just, 'don't come back,'" Sam corrected. "She said don't come back *all three of you*."

Her words kicked the breath out of them. Their eyes grew wide, looking from one to the other.

"Abby told me the night she ... she told me she had *talked to the Jabberwock*. And I just wrote it off that she was crazy, blew off what she said. But what if she really did talk to it?"

"What did the Jabberwock tell her?" Malachi wanted to know.

Charlie closed her eyes and tried to remember.

～

COTTON CAME in with boxes of pizza. Even cold, the smell was mouth-watering. But Jolene feared if she tried to eat a piece she'd dump the pepperoni and sausage in her lap. Her hands still hadn't stopped shaking. She reached up involuntarily and touched what she was certain must be bruises on her neck. She hadn't been able to face a mirror yet, didn't want to see the fingerprint marks on her skin.

One look at her and Stuart's faces and Cotton set the pizza down on the card table in his kitchen without opening the boxes.

"Appears the two of you had all the fun today. Want to talk about it before or after we eat?"

"After," Stuart said. "Or I won't eat."

Jolene nodded. She hadn't eaten anything since a huge breakfast in a Waffle House just outside Lexington this morning.

She sat there for an instant, stunned by the reality of it, of all that had happened in a single day. This morning had been a lifetime ago.

Food. Nourishment would help. She reached out with trembling fingers and picked up a slice of pizza.

Since neither she nor Stuart were particularly talkative, Cotton carried the conversational ball for most of the meal. He said he had found several boxes of his wife's genealogical records in the storage unit.

"She kept the most recent stuff at home — what's in storage is from a couple of years ago. I'll go through it later tonight." He cast a look at Stuart. "I'll have plenty of time."

"And that means?" Jolene said between bites. Once she started on the pizza she realized that she was ravenous. And as she ate, she settled, her nerves calmed. She stopped shaking.

Stuart said a single word. "Nightmares."

They'd told her about the bad dreams.

"You two plan to stay up all night — not even try to go to sleep?"

The two of them said yes at the same time with the perfect unison of a Greek chorus.

"Suit yourselves, but count me out. I've had more drama in my life today than … than *ever*. I will sleep like the dead."

They exchanged another look, but didn't challenge her.

Once Cotton finished eating, he wanted to hear what had happened, and the retelling of it stole Jolene's appetite so that she slid her last unfinished piece back into the box.

"Was it Reece Tibbits, the guy you saw blow up the road?" Cotton asked Stuart.

"What we saw was …" Stuart looked at Jolene for support and she tossed the look right back at him.

"Don't ask me!" She shivered involuntarily. "I have no idea what we saw. Was it a man? A real man? A *live* man … with bugs dropping out of his mouth? Ashy gray skin, blue lips, cold touch …"

"Are you saying they were—"

Jolene didn't mean to shout, but that's how it came out: "If you even whisper the word *zombie*, I will scream and scream and scream until I go crazy and drive you crazy with me!"

Silence flowed into the room after her outburst.

"They *weren't* holograms," Stuart inserted quietly. "That much we know. Beyond that ..."

Jolene felt all the energy and life suddenly drain out of her, water out a hole in a bucket.

"You fellas can stay up and dig through all the cans of worms we opened up today if that's what you're determined to do," she said. "But I'm fried. I need my beauty sleep. I have to get up early in the morning."

"Early ... to do what?" Cotton said.

"I want to get back out to Reece Tibbits's house first thing."

"Back?" Cotton was incredulous.

"Of course *back.*" She cut her eyes to Stuart. "What with one thing and another we were in a bit of a hurry to get out of there this afternoon — ran off and left the equipment. Remember? All the data from today at my father's house, the readings on those machines — that's the proof that'll bring the teeming hordes to Nowhere County. We can't just leave it sitting there."

She looked from one to the other.

"You don't have to go with me, I'll—"

"We're in this together," Stuart said.

Jolene tried not to look relieved. She'd been bluffing. She couldn't possibly go back to that house alone.

"I'm afraid I'm going to bail on you again," Cotton said. "I know the Tibbits place is where all the cool kids go, but I've got a hot date."

"With whom?" she asked.

"The Witch of Gideon."

Chapter Thirty-Six

"ABBY TOLD Thelma Jackson that the Jabberwock had 'whispered in her ear' — I remember now," Sam said. "Thelma was there when Abby came through that last time. She said Abby told her the Jabberwock told her 'the whole story.'"

"Abby's mind was gone," Charlie said. "She was babbling, but she did say that the Jabberwock was ... my *pet*."

That's why Abby had come for Charlie, why she had pretended to lock Merrie in the kiln — *would have* locked her in there if she could have. The others might not believe that, but Charlie did. Charlie had felt the hatred in the crazy eyes of the monster who'd been standing in the shadows of her little girl's bedroom holding a rifle. The others might grant her grace, might have told themselves that it had been a bluff all along, that Abby had never intended to harm the child. Charlie knew different. In her heart of hearts, she believed that Abby Clayton fully intended to pick Merrie up, carry her out into the backyard and lock her in an airless kiln. Would have done it if she could have. She only hid the little girl under the bed because by then Abby'd lost so much blood she was too weak to do what she'd intended to do.

Yes, Abby Clayton had been insane, had sustained brain damage courtesy of three rides on the Jabberwock. But in Charlie's mind, that didn't buy her out. No amount of mental instability was justification for smothering to death a three-year-old child.

Charlie didn't realize her thoughts must have been written on her face until Sam reached out and touched her hand. "I know you don't want to think about it."

"It's asking a lot," Malachi said gently. "But could you … would you *try* to remember all the details?"

"Okay," she said, shaky. "Give me a second."

Then she reached back down into the heart of darkness, found her way along shadowed corridors in her mind until she came to the door deep in the blackest corner of her soul. She turned the doorknob and went inside.

A MONSTER STEPS out of the shadows of Merrie's bedroom. She is a creature from all the horror movies, a spawn of hell — dirty, cut, bleeding, her face a mask of rage.

The eyes. Charlie can't tell the color, but even in the dim light, they radiate a hatred that is bottomless and unknowable. There is nothing, absolutely nothing that this creature won't do, no horror of which she is incapable. She had gone out there beyond all the boundaries of humanity and become a creature of the purest evil.

Charlie tries but can't picture what Abby Clayton had looked like when she first saw her, fuzzy blonde hair, face still raw from very recent adolescent acne. But beautiful with hope and love and joy and excitement. That girl was a person life had smiled on.

This creature is none of those things. She is bleeding or has bled out of every orifice of her body. Small streams of blood, not gushing, but surely the accumulated blood loss …

Bloody tears stream down her filthy cheeks. Her ears are bleeding, as is her nose, and the crotch of the scrub pants is a wet, black stain.

She'd suffered some kind of stroke or brain bleed or something because the left side of her face isn't lined up properly with the other side. Her voice is the sound of chains dragged across a metal floor. Cold and ragged and fearful in every way. The strip of light that slices into the room from the hallway lights the fire of rage on her face. Sparkles in her eyes.

The left side of her body doesn't appear to be affected by the stroke or whatever has happened in her brain. She holds the rifle firmly, finger on the trigger.

It takes several gasps before Charlie has enough air to speak.

"Where's Merrie? What have you done with my baby?"

"Ain't 'bout where she is. It's 'bout where she ain't and she ain't where she's supposed to be." Abby takes another shuffling step farther into the light. "Just like I ain't where I'm supposed to be — up Lexington with my boy."

"What have you done with—?"

"Shut up!"

The words ride a spray of blood out the creature's mouth.

"Ain't for you to be talkin'. You listen. You brung that monster down on us. Ain't no use denying it. I heard them whispering, the voices, saying the Jabberwock come to Nowhere County to play kiddie games with you and them others and have fun."

"What on earth are you talking—?"

"I said for you to shut your filthy witch's mouth!"

Abby advances another step.

"But you got yourself a sword, one of them 'vorpal blades' and you gonna use it on him. You gonna go looking for him in the woods behind that mirror thing where he hides. You gonna find him and kill him. Cut off his head — snicker snack — hold it up for everybody to *see. Then everything'll go back to the way it's supposed to be and I can go get to my baby."*

"Where is my little girl?"

CHARLIE HEARD herself repeat the words she'd said to Abby, demanding to know what Abby had done with Merrie, and she suddenly felt so nauseated she had to swallow rapidly to keep from throwing up.

The room had grayed out around her while she'd talked, but it snapped back into focus now and she was grateful for the smell of warm coffee and the faint strawberry scent of Sam's hair, noticed how it hung over her shoulders in cascades of red.

"Charlie …?" Sam asked.

"I'm okay." She shook it off, the skeins of the nightmare images clinging to her like a spiderweb when you run through one in the woods.

"So Abby said the Jabberwock came here to '*play kiddie games*' with you, that you were going to 'have fun together' — is that right?" Malachi asked. "She said *those words*?"

"Uh huh."

"That matches, it fits what the Jabberwock wrote on your blackboard. 'Stay here and *play with me*.'" Malachi paused and she could see the tumblers clicking into place. "So we were right about the *game* part, that this whole thing is some kind of game. But we were wrong about the Jabberwock 'grabbing random people' to play it. The Jabberwock told Abby he came here specifically for *you*. To play with you."

"And Thelma Jackson said Abby told her the Jabberwock would stay here until it 'got what it wanted,'" Sam said.

Charlie felt goosebumps spread out all over her body.

"The Jabberwock was looking for you specifically, Charlie," Malachi said, "but he took the whole county because he had to catch all the fish in the sea to get the one he wanted."

"Not just *me*," Charlie corrected. "He may have been 'the witch's' pet,' but Abby said he came here to play 'with you and them others.' And I think we know who those others are."

She looked from Sam to Malachi and back to Sam.

"Is it us, *the three of us*?" Sam's husky voice was barely a whisper.

"We played hide and seek in the woods, 'made it want.'" Charlie said the words as she thought them, as her mind made the connections. "That's what the Witch of Gideon said, and she warned us not to come back here 'all three' of us."

"You said it that first morning," Malachi said. "The morning after J-Day, you pointed out that this is *the first time* all three of us have been back in Nowhere County at the same time since graduation."

He shook his head, spoke the next words in wonder.

"Now we know the answer to 'why *now?*'"

Sam still backed up from it. "We don't *know*—"

"Yes, we do. It's been waiting for the three of us to be here together so—"

Charlie found herself backing up, too. "You *really* think—?"

"And you *don't*?" Malachi's voice had a hard edge. He looked from one to the other of them. "We can't keep dancing around the edges of this. We have to *own* it. The Jabberwock is about us." He pointed at Charlie. "You." Then at Sam. "You." And tapped his own chest. "And me."

"The Jabberwock has imprisoned Nowhere County ..." Charlie didn't have the air to finish, so Sam did it for her.

"... because it wants to play with us."

THE END

A Note from the Author

Thank you for reading *The Hanging Judge*.

If you enjoyed this book, you please consider writing a review on your favorite bookselling site so other readers might enjoy it too. Just a couple of sentences would mean a lot to me.

Thank you!

Ninie Hammon

A Note from the Author

About the Author

Ninie Hammon (rhymes with shiny, not skinny) grew up in Muleshoe, Texas, got a BA in English and theatre from Texas Tech University and snagged a job as a newspaper reporter. She didn't know a thing about journalism, but her editor said if she could write he could teach her the rest of it and if she couldn't write the rest of it didn't matter. She hung in there for a 25-year career as a journalist. As soon as she figured out that making up the facts was a whole lot more fun than reporting them, she turned to fiction and never looked back.

Ninie now writes suspense--every flavor except pistachio: psychological suspense, inspirational suspense, suspense thrillers, paranormal suspense, suspense mysteries.

In every book she keeps this promise to her Loyal Reader: "I will tell you a story in a distinctive voice you'll always recognize, about people as ordinary as you are--people who have been slammed by something they didn't sign on for, and now they must fight for their lives. Then smack in the middle of their everyday worlds, those people encounter the unexplainable--and it's always the game-changer."

Also By Ninie Hammon

Cornbread Mafia

Fire In The Hole

Blown' Up A Storm

Ridin' For A Fall

Nowhere, USA

The Jabberwock

Mad Dog

Trapped

The Hanging Judge

The Witch of Gideon

Blown Away

Nowhere People

Through The Canvas Series

Black Water

Red Web

Gold Promise

Blue Tears

The Taken Saga

The Taken

The Changed

The Hidden

The Saved

The Unexplainable Collection

Five Days in May

Black Sunshine

The Based on True Stories Collection

Home Grown

Sudan

When Butterflies Cry

The Knowing Series

The Knowing

The Deceiving

The Reckoning

The Fault

Stand-alone Psychological Thrillers

The Memory Closet

The Last Safe Place